# STREET SIGNS &
# SHADED GOODBYES

# Street Signs & Shaded Goodbyes

## Michael Lajoie

Reddington Press

To Hailey

&

To the former residents of
4 Eastmor Lane

It's not the same here without you.

Also by Michael Lajoie

*The Summit by the Sea*
*As Way Leads onto Way*

# Contents

September 1950

Camden, Maine

U.S.A.

# 1

The young couple smiled at each other over the rims of their glasses and sipped the cool Campari in the early evening heat. The lights were low and the door to the waterfront bar was propped open. Outside, the sun was setting fire to the sea. Inside, it was calm and quiet. The bartender was off doing dishes, and the woman and her husband had already paid and left a tip. Now, they were smiling and sipping and saying nothing.

There was something to be said about saying nothing. It was soothing to sit in silence with someone you loved while you drank it all in. It didn't matter if you were smitten with sadness or gaunt with grief. Your sighs were never-ending, and the feeling was always the same.

"What do you think, Vi?" the woman's husband said.

Violet raised an eyebrow. "About what?"

"Life."

She smirked. "You know already."

"Do I?"

"You ought to."

"Of course, I ought to. But it's more fun to ask."

"You're ridiculous..."

"No, I'm curious. What do you make of it?"

She let her gaze wander up and down the bar. Eventually, it settled back on her glass. She closed her eyes and drank some Campari. It was bitter and biting—all citrus and cynicism.

"Well?" her husband said.

"You know already..."

"How should I?"

"Because," she said, "we've lived enough life together to know what we make of it."

He grinned. "It's been one hell of a time."

"Which part?"

"All of it, I suppose."

"The Depression?"

He shrugged. "That wasn't so bad."

"The war?"

"That was much worse," he said. "To hell with every minute of that."

She nodded. "It was lonely in Hampton. I'm sure it was lonely in Italy, too."

"Italy was a good, strong drink," he said. "It had a bitter aftertaste."

"Like Campari?"

"A bit like Campari. A bit more like espresso."

She sipped and swallowed. "Thank God it's over."

"Yes." He took a drink and pursed his lips and looked like he had something else to say. She told him he could say it.

"No," he said. "I don't want to bring you down."

"You won't," she said. "I'm already down."

He hesitated.

"I mean it, Greg. What's the difference if we're both already thinking it?"

"I don't know," he said. "We could do without being so bitter about it."

"We've always been bitter about it," she said.

"Have we?"

"Well, maybe not always. For a while, we were sad."

"We're still sad."

"Yes, but we're more bitter now."

He stared into his glass. "How long has it been?"

"Long enough."

"How long is that?"

She thought for a moment. "Six years, give or take. Bill died in '44."

"And we moved here in '45?"

"In the fall of '45, yeah. It wasn't long after you got back."

Greg drank. "And how do you feel about it?"

"Pretty numb," she said. "But that's nothing new."

"No," he said. "That's nothing new at all."

She finished her Campari and shook her head.

"What is it?"

"It's bitter," she said. "It's very bitter."

"The Campari?"

"No," she said. "Life."

He drained what was left in his glass. "Yeah," he said. "It sure as hell is…"

She sighed, looking toward the door. "Should we move on?"

He shrugged. "We might as well."

Outside the bar, it was just as calm and just as quiet. The tide was low and the sun was sinking over the docks. The bay was entirely golden.

Greg shielded his eyes. "Where should we go?"

"Back home?"

"Not yet. It's too nice of a night."

"Downtown?"

He offered her his hand. "Why not?"

"All right."

They made for the boardwalk. Violet stopped.

"Change your mind?" Greg said.

"No," she said. "I just wonder if we should go back for Izzy."

"She should be fine," he said. "We let her out after she ate."

Violet glanced at his watch.

"Hey," he said, and kissed her cheek. "She should be fine."

"I know, I know—but you know how I get."

"Don't worry about it. She was sleeping when we left and she'll be sleeping when we get back. That's all she does nowadays."

"You're right," Violet said. "She's our sleepy girl."

Greg squeezed her hand. "Even if she does wake up before we get back, she knows better than to go."

"I hope she does. She's old, Greg."

"I know she is," he said. "But she knows not to go while we're gone. She'll be fine. We'll see her when we get back."

They followed the boardwalk to the sidewalk, which led onto Main Street. The rolling ridges of the Camden Hills rose above the town, gazing down at the flat rooves and sand-colored awnings of the various shops and restaurants. The shops were mostly closed, and the restaurants were about as empty as the waterfront bar. Waiters with rolled-up sleeves were standing by with trays of food and were serving drinks to the people sitting outside.

On the east side of Main Street was the library and a park that overlooked the harbor. It was edged with bushes and beach roses and spindly white birches that swayed softly in the warm evening breeze. Out in the bay, the water was smooth and still. The sailboats were bobbing in their moorings, and the horizon was aflame with the sunset. They sat on a bench and watched a pair of cormorants drying their wings on a rock beside the water. They were beautiful birds, and this was a beautiful park. Violet smiled. There was so much wrong with the world, but right now, everything seemed all right.

Greg glanced back in the direction of the library. "Well, back to work tomorrow…"

"Yes," Violet said. "But then you have the next two off."

"Do we have any plans?"

"Only if we make them."

"Let's get away somewhere," he said. "It's been a while since we've gotten away."

"What about Izzy?"

"We'll bring her along. It'll be good for her, too."

"We'll have to find someplace that takes dogs."

"There are places. We'll find one."

She grinned. "Do you have somewhere in mind?"

He shrugged.

"You do," she said. "Where?"

"I don't know," he said. "It's just an idea. Kind of a crazy idea, to be honest."

"Where?"

"Hampton."

Her grin faded. "New Hampshire?"

He laughed and shook his head. "I told you it was crazy."

"It's not crazy," she said. "It's..." She trailed off, staring at the bay. "What makes you want to go back?"

"You know, I'm not really sure. I've just been thinking about it."

"About what?"

"Whether anything's changed."

"There's only one way to find out," she said. "But I don't know if I want to."

"You don't want to go back?"

She hesitated. "I don't know. There's a reason why we left."

"Do you think we would've left if Bill had come back?"

"Probably not."

"I wonder if he would've left."

"I doubt it."

"You don't think he would've moved to Portsmouth?"

"I don't know. Maybe he would've." She sighed. "It's hard to say."

"I think he would've," Greg said. "He loved it there. We did, too." He smiled. "Remember Al Mare's on State Street?"

"Of course, I do," she said. It was the restaurant where she had first tried Campari. "Some of the best Italian food around."

"You haven't been to Italy..."

"No," she said. "I was taking care of Izzy in Hampton."

"It's a good thing you were. She would've had nobody else."

"I wish she still had Bill. You think she knows he's really gone?"

"I'm sure she does. She's a smart dog."

"We lost him, but I'm happy we still have her. I hope we've made him proud."

"You know we have, Vi."

"I know, but I still hope."

They were both staring at the bay. The light was almost gone.

"We ought to take her back," Greg said. "At least once, before she dies."

Violet winced at the approaching night. "Goddammit, Greg…"

"We really should," he said. "She's done so much for us. It's the kindest thing we can do in return."

She said nothing, knowing he was right but not wanting to think about it. Her brother was gone, and his old black dog was going to die. It was the truth but it was hell to think about. She felt around the bench for Greg's hand.

He found hers and squeezed it gently. When he spoke, his voice was sad and kind. "Think about it," he said. "That's all I'm asking you to do."

She squeezed his hand back. "It's getting dark," she said. "Let's go home."

# 2

They walked back to their house on Chestnut Street and let Izzy out when they got in. After, they put her to bed and went to bed themselves. There was sweetness beneath the sheets and peace through sleep. Everything was assuaged overnight.

The alarm went off the next morning at half past six. Greg shut it off with a groan and sat up in bed. He stretched and went to the bathroom for a shower. Izzy stirred at the foot of the bed as he left the room, and Violet heard her stand and shake off her drowsiness. She plodded over to Violet's side of the bed and nudged the covers with her snout.

"Well, good morning," Violet mumbled.

Izzy wagged her tail. There was love and light in her old brown eyes. For as long as Violet could remember, it had always been there. She reached out to pat Izzy's head, and Izzy kissed her hand. Violet smiled, heaving herself out of bed.

The wood floor creaked a greeting as they made their way out of the bedroom and down the hall. They passed the bathroom and through the dining room, then paused in the kitchen. Izzy whimpered impatiently at the back door.

"Easy, easy," Violet said, unlocking it. She opened the door and went out first, gesturing for Izzy to follow. Izzy wobbled down the steps with an elderly sigh, huffing in quiet triumph when she reached the bottom.

Violet patted her side. "Good girl..."

She waited, barefoot, in the grass as Izzy searched the back-yard for a spot to do her business. It was a serene and secluded place, enclosed by hedges and presided over by pine trees. In the middle of the yard were a few arborvitaes, a birdbath, and a dew-covered cluster of rosebushes. Nearby was a little wooden table and a matching set of chairs, where she and Greg often sat in the evenings.

Izzy finished her business and came trotting back, and the two of them went up the steps together. At the top, Violet patted her again and let her inside. She closed the door, turned on the lights in the kitchen, and went to the cabinet for Izzy's bowl. Izzy sat on the doormat, watching her intently.

Violet took the bowl to the big bag of dry food leaning against the refrigerator, filling it to the brim with little brown pellets. She dampened the food with some tap water and set the bowl by Izzy's front paws. Izzy looked down at it, then back up at her.

"What do you say?" Violet asked.

Izzy whimpered, and Violet beamed.

"Oh, good girl. Go ahead."

Izzy ate ravenously, finishing her breakfast in a matter of minutes. She licked her chops and wandered around the kitchen, sniffing the floor for any overnight changes. When she was through, she returned to her bowl and inspected it for any bits of food that she might have missed while she was eating. She licked it clean and wagged her tail. Violet scratched her back and stroked her ears.

Greg came in, looking clean-shaven and sharply-dressed. His hair was combed and his thin pencil mustache was neatly-trimmed. His shirt and slacks were pressed, and his tie was straight and dimpled. Violet always thought he would look more like a librarian if he wore glasses. Without them, he looked a bit like Errol Flynn. His eyes were just as wise and just as bright.

"Morning, girls," he said. He sat at the table and Izzy rested her head on his knee.

"Morning." Violet brought him a banana and a bowl of shredded wheat. He poured the milk himself and handed the bottle back to her.

Izzy eyed the banana and lifted her head. Greg covered her eyes with his hand. She peeked at him through the gaps in his fingers.

"Hey," he said, peeling the banana. "Didn't you already have breakfast?"

Violet laughed. "You know how she is. She ate so fast that she probably forgot..."

"In that case," Greg said. He broke off the tip of the banana and offered it to her. She accepted it gently and lay at his feet. He sliced up the rest of the banana with the handle of his spoon, then added it to his cereal. When he finished the bowl, he checked his watch.

Violet glanced at the clock above the sink. It was a quarter past seven.

Greg got up from the table and stretched. His shift at the library started at eight, and it took him about twenty minutes to walk there. They had a car—a black '46 Ford—but he left it at home for Violet to use during the day. She'd offered to drive him to work before, but he always declined. The walk was good for him, he said. It cleared his mind and prepared him for the next eight hours of sitting.

"All right, you two," he said. He smiled down at Izzy and kissed Violet goodbye.

She kissed him back. "See you tonight."

He left out the front door, bound for the sidewalk. Violet smiled at him from the doorway. After he had gone, she went back to the kitchen and switched on the coffeemaker. Izzy followed her and settled down on the doormat for a nap. Violet showered while the coffee brewed and toweled off to the smell of dark roast. She dressed, put her hair up, and returned to the kitchen to pour herself a cup. She savored the taste. It was black and strong.

She roused Izzy from her nap, opened the back door, and helped her down the steps. Izzy set out into the yard, sniffing and snuffling through the grass. While she explored, Violet brought her coffee to the little wooden table by the rosebushes and sat in one of the matching chairs. She watched the steam billow up and out of the mug, then shifted her gaze to Izzy. She was fourteen. That was old for a dog.

Bill had gotten her when she was just a puppy, from a breeder in Quebec. She had come with the name *Ici*, which meant "here" in French—and so, he had called her "Izzy." Violet and Greg had first met her when she was a year old, in 1937.

They had all grown up in a coastal town in northeastern Massachusetts. Bill was four years older than Violet, and he had graduated high school at the start of the Depression. By the time she and Greg had graduated, he had moved to New Hampshire and built himself a life there. He had a house on the outskirts of town and a job at a small airfield, where he fixed and flew airplanes. At their wedding, he had told them about his new puppy and invited them up for a visit.

They had visited once, then again, then many other times after that. Bill had taken them flying every time. Greg had loved it. He had been struggling to find work in Massachusetts, and asked Bill if he would teach him how to fly.

"I'll do you one better," Bill had told him. "How'd you like a job?"

Violet smiled, sipping her coffee. He had been a damned good brother, taking them in like that. They had made themselves a home in Hampton—the three of them and their black Labrador retriever. Bill was their guiding light through the Depression. He hadn't even charged them rent. The only thing he had asked was for Violet to watch his dog if he ever went away. She had told him she would, and he called on her for that favor in the spring of 1942.

She had known the conversation had been coming since the attack on Pearl Harbor. The world was at war and there was no avoiding it, especially now that the US was involved. Bill had already told her he didn't want to be drafted. Greg didn't want to be, either. The two of them were going to enlist in the Air Force.

At the time, she wasn't sure how to feel about it. She figured they'd be safer in the Air Force than they would be in the Army. They could fly better than anyone she knew. Maybe they would be able to outfly the bullets. She hadn't known then about dogfights or engine failures or anti-aircraft artillery. She had thought vaguely about their possibility, but hadn't seriously considered them.

But Bill and Greg were going, and she and Izzy were staying. She would look after her until the two of them came back—and they would come back. She was sure of it.

She remembered the three of them had gone out to dinner, not long after Bill and Greg had decided to enlist. They had driven into Portsmouth and parked by the South Mill Pond, then walked the rest of the way to Al Mare's on State Street. They sat outside on the terrace and ordered a bottle of Campari. It was beautifully bitter. They drank half of it before glancing through their menus for something to eat.

"What do you think, Greg?" Bill said.

Greg scratched his mustache. "Some soup, maybe. I like the sound of their bisque."

"That does sound good." He nodded at Violet. "You hungry, Vi?"

She wasn't really, but she said she was. "Does the bisque come with bread?"

Greg nodded.

"Then I'll have some of your bread."

"You sure you don't want anything else?"

She shook her head. "That'll be enough for me."

Greg paused and pointed at the menu. "I think the caprese salad comes with bread, if you want that."

Bill chuckled and took a drink.

"What?" Greg said.

"You just want your bread."

"No, I just want to make sure she has enough to eat..." He smirked. "And that I do, too."

"I'll order bread with my chicken cannelloni," Bill said. "And another bottle of Campari. Then we can all share."

"Good man," Greg said, and Violet smiled at both of them.

"You're both good men," she said.

"Oh, boy." Bill raised his glass. "Here's Violet, the sentimentalist..."

"I mean it," she said. "You're both damned good men, and I'm happy to have you." Under the table, Greg nudged her leg and offered her his hand. She held it and went on. "I really hope we get to do this again. Something inside me says we won't."

"What, have a drink?" Bill said. "You can drink all you want when we're away. Anything from my cabinet is yours. Have whatever you like." He winked. "Nothing for Izzy, though, all right?"

She managed a laugh. "No, I meant—"

"I know what you meant," Bill said.

They were silent. Violet took a long sip of Campari.

Greg squeezed her hand. "I'm sure we'll get to," he said. "It shouldn't take too long to bring this thing to an end."

"Not long at all," Bill said. "We have the British and the Soviets—"

"—and what's left of the French," Greg added.

"Shame we don't have all of the French," Bill said. "What'd they go and get invaded for? They held the Germans off fine before Versailles. What the hell changed?"

Greg shrugged. "Apparently, a hell of a lot."

"Maybe they got complacent," Bill said. "The world has a nasty habit of humbling you as soon as you get complacent. That sort of thing happens all the time."

"Remind me to never get complacent," Violet said.

They both stared at her.

"What?" she said. "I want both of you home in a few years' time. The world isn't going to humble me. Not if I can help it."

Greg squeezed her hand again. "You're not complacent, Vi. None of us are."

"I might be a little," Bill said.

"Shut up," Greg said. "You and I are going away to fight this war, and it'll be over before we all know it."

Violet sighed. "I like the sound of that."

"I do, too," Bill said. "Matter of fact, let's drink to it." He raised his glass and waited for them to do the same.

"Cheers," Greg said, and drank.

"Cheers," Bill said, and looked at Violet.

Violet looked at both of them and willed herself to smile. She didn't know it then, but that night was the end and the beginning of so many things.

"Cheers," she said, and drank the Campari down. Its bitterness long afterward remained.

# 3

Violet took her last sip of coffee and looked down, realizing that Izzy had curled up by her feet. She tapped one of her paws with her foot.

"What do you think, sweet girl?"

Izzy cocked her head.

"You want to go for a walk?"

She got up with some difficulty and did her best to shake off her age. Her tail was a blur.

"All right," Violet said, getting up herself. She helped Izzy back inside and set her coffee mug in the sink. Izzy waited for her by the coatrack next to the front door, where her leash was hanging. She stayed still while Violet fastened it to her collar, whining eagerly.

"I know, I know," Violet said, selecting a stylish sunhat from the coatrack. She put it on at a tilt and shut the door behind them. They descended the front steps with care, pausing at the bottom so that Izzy could catch her breath. They took it slow on their way to the sidewalk and set off down Chestnut Street.

She quite liked the stretch of road that she and Greg lived on. The white clapboard houses were quaint and simple, with stately winged eagles affixed over their front doors. The trees in their yards were old and tall, and had doubtless been standing for far longer than the houses had. Their limbs and leaves loomed overhead, casting swaying shadows on the street. Between the street and the sidewalk stretched a long length of grass that was interrupted now and again by the houses' brick-laid driveways. Along this length of grass lay several things, all interspersed: green four-legged mailboxes, dormant spire-like lampposts, and speed limit signs reading *25 MPH*.

There were no cars on the street and no other people on the sidewalk. There were, instead, sparrows in the trees and squirrels scurrying up their antiquated trunks. Izzy observed them, ears perked, but made no effort to pull. She hardly ever pulled on her leash these days, and it hung slack in Violet's hand.

They strolled on. Eventually, Violet got to thinking about Hampton and the way it was when Bill and Greg were in Italy. Bill's house had felt very empty. She had hung two blue stars in the window facing the road—to let the world know that its war had taken her brother and husband away. As long as the stars were blue, there was hope that the world would send them home. They both stayed blue for a year. She remembered the day Bill's turned gold.

It was one of those gray days with no distinguishable dawn. The sky was as bleak as the telegram from Western Union. It was delivered by a man in uniform. His eyes were dark and deadpan. She stared at them long and hard.

*Someone you love is dead,* they said.

*I know,* hers answered. *Now get the hell off my porch.*

He handed her the telegram and strode back to his motorbike. Its saddlebags were bulging with other bad news. He sped off down Bill's driveway, turning the dirt to dust as he went.

Violet opened the telegram. Its text was sparse and unsympathetic:

MRS. EASTMOR

THE SECRETARY OF WAR DESIRES ME TO EXPRESS HIS DEEP REGRET THAT YOUR BROTHER CPL WILLIAM T. MASLOW HAS BEEN REPORTED KILLED IN ACTION OVER ITALY ON 25 APRIL 1944.

THE ADJUTANT GENERAL

That was it. That was all there was.

Another telegram arrived a week later. She thanked God that it was from Greg and not about him.

DEAR VIOLET

HEARD ABOUT BILL. WISH I COULD FLY HOME. HOPEFULLY SOON. THE COFFEE HERE IS BITTER AND SO IS THE CAMPARI. ALL MY LOVE TO YOU AND IZZY.

ALWAYS

GREG

She remembered how long it took for her to take down one of the blue stars in the window. Replacing it with a gold one felt like admitting defeat. She didn't care that the Allies were winning the war. Bill was dead. Her brother was lost.

His house had felt empty before, but it was worse now that she knew he was gone. Her days were sustained by coffee and Campari, and there was fog and mist and rain. When she ran out of Campari, she drank gin and tonics instead. She tried buying more Campari, but it was no use. The war had made Italian liquor almost impossible to find.

She spent as much time away from Hampton as possible. The pain was numbing, and she hardly knew her home. She and Izzy would take long drives in Bill's car. They would stop for gas in Portsmouth before following Route One over the bridge and into Maine. From there, they would drive for hours. Violet would stare at the lonely houses of the coastal towns. There were blue stars and gold stars in so many of the windows. The blue stars were always disappearing, and the gold stars were quick to take their place. It made her grimace. The world seemed so keen to move on.

She drove and drove—only stopping if they were low on fuel, or if Izzy needed to get out to do her business. If they left Portsmouth with a full tank of gas, they usually needed to fill up again in Rockport or Camden. Rockport was a harbor town, and it was very beautiful. Camden was even more beautiful—nestled at the base of the hills that rolled like waves and tumbled, headlong, into the sea.

There was a gas station on Elm Street, in the heart of downtown Camden. From the pump, Violet could see the sparsely-forested shoulder of the hill called Mt. Battie. An old carriage road that had since become a hiking trail provided direct access to the top. She and Izzy went up once, after getting gas. It was a steep climb, but she didn't mind it. Izzy, much younger at the time, didn't mind it, either.

The summit was revered as the place where Edna St. Vincent Millay had written some of her most famous poetry. She had grown up in Camden but had moved to New York City. One of her books had won the Pulitzer Prize, sometime before the war. Violet had read it during the Depression, but she couldn't remember what it was called. She remembered it was romantic and rebellious, though—and overall, quite good. There was a plaque bolted to the bedrock in honor of her work.

Not far from the plaque stood a stone watchtower—a memorial to the lives that had been lost during the First World War. Violet and Izzy ascended the spiral staircase and marveled at the view from the platform. Camden was spread out before them, alongside the shimmering bay. The white wakes of boats streaked past the lighthouse on Curtis Island, headed for the vastness of the open sea. The clouds overhead were fluffed and feathered, and the ocean went on and on beneath the unending sky.

It was one of the prettiest views she had ever seen, and she regretted the fact that Bill never got to see it. She swore to herself that she would take Greg up as soon as the war ended. A year later, when he got home from Italy, she did.

He didn't say much on the hike up the old carriage road, and she asked him what he thought at the top. He leaned against the crenellations of the stone watchtower, quietly catching his breath. Izzy sat at his feet. He patted her gratefully.

"That was one hell of a climb," he said, wiping the sweat from his forehead. He grinned, gazing out at all of it. "But this is pretty damned incredible..."

"I knew you'd love it." She beamed and held his hand and didn't care that it was sweaty. "Izzy loves it, too."

Greg admired the view awhile longer. "What do you say we come up here more often?"

Violet kissed his cheek. "I'd like that," she said. "I'd like that a lot."

She blinked and the memory faded. After several other visits to Camden, they had decided to make it their permanent home. Greg's stint in the Air Force had made them eligible to receive benefits from the G.I. Bill, which helped them buy their house on Chestnut Street. They emptied Bill's old house and put it up for sale. When it sold, they left Hampton behind. They hadn't been back since. Bill had been dead for six years.

She looked down at Izzy, wondering if she knew what had happened to him. He had gone away one day and she had never seen him again. In the meantime, she had grown old. Her days were now numbered—and diminishing.

Violet stopped on the sidewalk and knelt down beside her. Izzy's joints were creaky and occasionally unsteady, and her elbows were scuffed and calloused from her frequent naps on the floor. Her black fur was streaked and spotted with white. Her eyes were the youngest part of her. They always had been. Their love and light refused to fade.

Violet looked into them. "Bill's dead," she said softly. "You know that, don't you?"

Izzy sniffed the air and sighed.

Violet wrapped her arms around her. When she drew back, there were tears on her cheeks. Izzy kissed them away.

# 4

When they got back home, Violet had another cup of coffee and Izzy settled down for a nap. She drank it at the kitchen table, feeling increasingly restless, and decided she still wanted to walk. She patted Izzy awake and asked her if she wanted to go. Izzy yawned and closed her eyes again. Violet kissed her snout and let her be.

She readjusted her sunhat and set out once more. Chestnut Street was just as idyllic in the other direction. The sidewalk took her downtown, where a steady stream of traffic was crawling down Elm Street. She waited for a gap in the cars before hurrying across, holding her hat to her head.

On the corner of Elm and Mechanic Street was a little grocery store. There was a produce display in the window and a newspaper rack just outside the door. A few tables were set up on the sidewalk, and an old man was reading a newspaper at one of them. He took a puff from his cigarette and turned the page. Violet smiled at where he was sitting. She had sat there with Izzy countless times, back when they used to visit Camden during the war. After they stopped for gas, she would buy an apple for the two of them and they would alternate taking bites. People used to think that was the funniest thing. It was nice to see them smile—especially when, at the time, she hardly ever did.

She strolled past Mechanic Street's many flat-rooved buildings, rounded a bend, and then came upon its intersection with Washington Street. She turned onto Washington Street and the road narrowed, giving way to a footbridge that was built by the Works Progress Administration. Beneath the footbridge was a dam that thinned the flow of the Megunticook River. The river was calm and languid, but its current was only occasionally contained. It spilled over the dam every spring, and any other time of the year you could hear it rushing after a good rain. It ran on for quite a distance, disappearing under the town, until it reemerged in the harbor and coursed out into the bay.

Violet paused on the footbridge, contemplating the water. Eventually, her mind meandered and she was once again caught up in her memories. She thought about Hampton and about how hard it had been to say goodbye. She didn't know what to think when Bill's house sold. She knew a house was just a house without the people that made it a home, but that didn't make it any easier to leave. On the day they moved out, she had stood at the threshold of every room to take it all in. Greg and Izzy had waited outside. She had turned off all the lights, picked up her suitcase, and backed out the door. It was a silent farewell. Violet closed her eyes, hating how much it still hurt to remember.

She thought about Bill's house and everything it had meant to her. It was an old colonial homestead that overlooked a field and a long dirt driveway. Nearby was the Blake Farm and the Wayside Farm, and the stately white house that had once belonged to Simon Lane. It was quaint and very quiet, a perfect reflection of

Hampton's forested far reaches. In the evenings, deer traversed the field from the woods across the road. In the mornings, light streamed in through the windows, streaking the walls with an occasional rainbow and warming the floors for paws and bare feet. The brightness was like butterscotch, and there were few things as sweet as a still and early morning.

There were mornings like that in Camden, but their house on Chestnut Street was almost always in the shade. That was all right, though. The shade wasn't so bad when you were with someone you loved. When you weren't, or when you had lost them, it was one of the loneliest feelings in the world. Sometimes, even the light was lonely. She remembered when Bill died how much she had preferred the shade. The sun was a glaring reminder of how much happier she had been before her home and her heart had grown estranged.

Violet lifted her gaze and left the footbridge, feeling a little low. Washington Street ended at Elm Street, and she crossed over to the village green. There was a flagpole in the center, surrounded by benches and beach roses. People were sitting on the benches and on blankets in the grass. Some of them had young children. A few of them had dogs.

Violet thought of Izzy and sighed, knowing that they ought to take her back to Hampton. Greg was right—after everything she had done for them, taking her back home was the kindest thing they could do. A trip to Hampton wasn't anything she wanted, but this wasn't about her. This was about Izzy. Maybe they could stay in Portsmouth and it wouldn't be so bad. Again, Violet sighed. She wondered if Izzy was still sleeping and figured she probably was. In the years since Bill died, she had gotten so old.

From the village green, Violet walked back to Chestnut Street and followed it home. It was chilly beneath the shade of the trees, and she found herself searching for the sun the entire time. It appeared, at last, when she reached their driveway. She stood for a moment in its warmth, then went inside. Izzy was still fast asleep on the kitchen floor.

She made lunch, did the dishes, and started thinking about what to make for dinner. Izzy slept through all of it. She didn't wake up until half past four, when Greg knocked on the front door and let himself in.

"Hello, hello," he said, as Izzy trotted over to him. He scratched her head and patted her side. "You're nice and warm, girl. Have you been sleeping?"

"All day," Violet said, from the stove. She had just put a pot of pasta on to boil.

"All day?" Greg said, tussling Izzy's fur. He straightened up and peered at the pot. "What kind of sauce are you thinking?"

"Haven't decided yet," she said. "What are you in the mood for?"

"How about alfredo? I'll grate the cheese."

She grinned. "Sounds good to me."

He brought her the cream from the refrigerator and reached around her to fetch the cheese grater from the drawer. Violet kissed him. "How was work?"

"The same," he said. "Books are books and readers are readers." He unwrapped the wedge of parmesan and began grating it into a bowl. "Sometimes I wish they were a little more interesting."

Violet rummaged around in the cabinets for another pot and set it atop one of the burners. She measured out some flour and butter and let the mixture sit over low heat. "I hear you," she said. "My day was pretty quiet, too."

"What'd you do?"

"Took Izzy out in the morning. That was nice. When we got back, she went down for a nap. That nap lasted all day."

Greg chuckled and shook his head. "What a life…" He put the grater down for a second to loosen his tie and roll up his sleeves. "How much cheese do you want?"

She glanced at the bowl. "About half of that wedge should be fine. I think there's still some of that good bread left in the pantry, too."

"Oh, really?"

"Oh, yes."

"Do we have tomatoes?"

"We should."

"Garlic?"

"Mhm."

"What about balsamic vinegar?"

"I think we do…"

"Then I think I'll make some bruschetta. What do you think?"

Violet covered the pasta and added some cream to the roux. "I'll grate the rest of the cheese," she said. "You work your magic."

"Yes, ma'am." He handed her the cheese grater and kissed her cheek.

Over the course of fifteen minutes, their simple meal came together. Izzy watched it come to fruition. Before they started eating, Violet fed her. She finished quickly and resumed watching them. Food seemed to be the only thing that kept her awake. It was a delicious meal. The alfredo sauce was rich and creamy over the pasta, and the bruschetta was bright and crisp over the bread. When their plates were empty, Greg brought them to the sink. He returned to the table with two glasses and three quarters of a bottle of Campari. Violet smiled as he poured.

He glanced toward the back door. "Want to sit outside?"

"Sure."

They took Izzy out with them and set their glasses down on the table by the rosebushes. She lay in the grass, sniffing the flowers. The advancing twilight made them tremble and blush.

"I've always loved roses," Violet said. She bent down and picked up a fallen petal. It was silky between her fingers. "I wish they bloomed forever."

"Me, too," Greg said. "But I'm not surprised they don't."

"No?"

"Not really."

"Why's that?"

"Few good things ever last."

"Some things last," she said.

"Yes, some things do." He winked at her and raised his glass. "Like love."

"Like love," she said, and winked back.

They drank. Down in the grass, Izzy yawned. Violet patted her to keep her awake.

"So sleepy," Greg remarked.

Violet stroked her ears. "Too sleepy," she said. "It makes me nervous."

"Don't think too much of it," he said. "She's just getting old."

"I know she is, but it still makes me nervous."

"She's all right, Vi. She'd let us know if she wasn't."

"Yeah, I know."

He sipped his Campari and set it on the table. "You're thinking," he observed.

"A little."

"About what?"

"Hampton, to be honest."

He turned and looked at her from his chair. "What about it?"

She took a deep breath. "We should probably go back."

"Yeah?"

"Yeah."

"What makes you say that?"

"Her," she said. "She has me worried."

"Violet," Greg said.

"I mean it, Greg. She slept all day and she's been sleeping more and more. If we're going to bring her home, we should probably do it soon."

"I thought you didn't want to go."

"I'll never want to go," she said. "But I know we still should—for her, if not for anyone else." She took a sip of Campari. "Could we stay in Portsmouth? I've never minded it there."

"Absolutely, we can. We'll find a place there tomorrow afternoon."

"After you get out of work?"

He nodded. "It's not too long of a drive. Three hours, if I remember right—straight down Route One."

She drank and stared at the roses, perplexed by their perishable beauty. "Why did he have to die?"

Greg heaved a sigh. "Why does anyone have to die?"

"I don't know," she said.

"I don't, either. They say everything happens for a reason, but God only knows what that reason is."

"They do say that, don't they?"

"I've heard it, once or twice."

"You know what else they say?"

"What's that?"

"That time heals all wounds." She took a drink.

Greg did, too. "What do you make of that?" he asked.

"I think you know."

"Tell me, anyway."

"I think it's a lie," Violet said. "I think whoever said that never lost anybody. I think time makes things hurt worse." She took another drink and grimaced. "What do you think about it?"

"I don't know," Greg said. "I'd like to think there's more to it, but I don't know if there is."

"What else would there be?"

"I don't know," he said again. "I think whoever said it must've been feeling that way. Time healed their wounds—it just hasn't healed ours. Who knows, maybe it will someday."

She grinned. "You're one hell of an optimist."

"Someone has to be..."

Her gaze settled on Izzy, who was sleeping now in the grass. "She is. We're both down, but she brings us up."

"She's a good girl," Greg said. "She's loved to pieces, and she knows it."

"I wish she wasn't so old."

"Yeah, so do I. But you know, she seems to be at peace with it."

"She seems to be at peace with a lot of things," Violet said. "All these years, and I still haven't learned how she does it."

"Peace through life and peace with death," Greg mused. "To think a dog solved the great mystery…"

"I'm happy she's ours."

Greg smiled. "I am, too."

They touched glasses in the twilight as Izzy slept on in the grass. The sun was setting on the roses. The Campari was crimson in the dusk.

# 5

The following morning, Greg took the car to work. They had decided in bed that he would get gas on his way home from the library. Violet would have their bags packed and ready for when he got back.

She showered, brewed a pot of coffee, and brought a steaming mug with her to the bedroom. Izzy followed her, laying down at the foot of the bed. She watched Violet go into the closet and pull a pair of suitcases down from the shelf. Violet heaved them onto the bed and propped them open. Dust clung to the edges of their felt-lined interiors, and she cleared it away.

She packed her suitcase first, selecting a few dresses from the coat hangers in the closet and laying them neatly within. They were ocean-blue and olive-green, with daisy-white buttons above the waist and discreet tie-back belts. All of them had matching sunhats, and she stacked them inside one another so they would take up less space. She considered not bringing them, but she loved the way she looked in a sunhat—and she knew Greg did, too.

She turned and admired his smiling face in one of the black-and-white photographs atop the dresser. It had been taken fifteen years ago, on their wedding day. They both looked so young, so happy—despite the fact that at the time, they were weathering the Depression. Bill had been there, and he had told them about Izzy. That was when he had first invited them up to fly.

There was a photo of him on the dresser, too. In it, he was standing beside a biplane in Hampton, clad in a leather jacket and scarf. He held a leash in his hand, which was very clearly keeping a little black puppy from wandering out of the shot. She showed the photo to Izzy, who nudged it curiously with her nose. Violet wiped the smudge away and turned the frame over in her hands. With a sigh, she removed the backing board. An old telegram was folded and pressed against the photo within.

She took it out and unfolded it. It had been sent from Maxwell Field in Montgomery, Alabama:

VIOLET

SHIPPING OFF TO THE FIGHT. GREG IS TOO. NEW OR-DERS TO BOOT. KEEP YOUR HEAD UP FOR IZZY AND FOR ALL OF US.

TAKE CARE SIS

BILL

She studied the words on the crinkled yellow paper, know-ing that her brother had chosen them carefully. All mail sent by servicemen during the war was reviewed by military censors, and she had received many telegrams with some of the sentences blacked-out. The rationale for this, she assumed, was to prevent anything useful from falling into enemy hands. She understood it, but she hated it. If not for Bill's double entendre, she would've been kept in the dark.

*New orders to boot,* he had written.

New orders to *the* boot—the shoe-shaped Italian peninsula.

*Clever, Bill,* she thought. *Very clever.*

She refolded the telegram and put it back in the frame, returning the photo to its place on the dresser. There were three others alongside it, all bordered by tarnished brass. In the next, the little black puppy had grown into a big black dog. It was sitting in the same airfield in Hampton, once again at Bill's feet. Violet and Greg were standing on either side of them, smiling wide. They had made such a living in that airfield. Bill and Greg and the other pilots would take people up for rides. It had been nice, during the Depression, to give people that kind of escape. Those were good days. She wished they had lasted longer.

The next two photos were of Greg and had been taken during the war. In one of them, he stood solo beside an airplane that bore Violet's name. She grinned. He looked very handsome in his uniform, with his hand resting on the plane's nose. In the other, he was sitting in a restaurant in Italy. By then, Bill had died and countless others had, too. Greg was smiling, but his gaze was gaunt and hollow. He was at a table with four other airmen, raising his glass to the camera.

Violet considered the photograph. It showed her all of the things about the war that her husband talked about—the remnants of a delicious meal, the latter half of an evening cocktail, and the smiling faces of fallen friends. But it showed her nothing else, and the unknown unnerved her. She swallowed and stepped away. Greg's suitcase lay empty on the bed.

She imagined, during the war, that her eyes had often mirrored his. She had done her best to grimace through her grief, numb and nonchalant to all of it. If Greg had been home, he would've been able to tell she was hurting—but he hadn't been, and that was just the way it was. Izzy had almost certainly been able to tell. Fake smiles and feigned indifference meant absolutely nothing to her. She was a dog, after all. Empathy was her everything. Most of the time, her love had kept the loneliness at bay.

When it hadn't, Violet surrendered herself to the sadness and hid herself away. She would drive into Portsmouth on her own, bound for Al Mare's and a melancholy dinner. It rained hard the spring that Bill died, and when it wasn't raining, it was drizzly and foggy and gray. Seating on the terrace opened late, but even after it did, she still sat inside. The low lighting and live jazz made friends with her indigo mood, encouraging her to feel what she felt as she mourned with the music. There were meditative renditions of songs she knew and songs she didn't—but she came to know them all as spring made its way into summer, and as summer faded slowly into fall. 1944 was a hell of a year. So was the first half of 1945. She spent many dismal nights at Al Mare's. A gin and tonic usually kept her company.

She recalled there had been plenty of people at the restaurant, but they had mostly kept to themselves. They had been just like her—lonely women with their doubts and their drinks and their downcast eyes. They were wives and they were sisters, and they had each lost something different to the war. For some, it was love. For others, it was hope. For all of them, it was a piece of the place they called home. There was no getting that back. Violet wished there was, but there wasn't. The legacy of their loss was grief everlasting.

Grief was cold and isolating. It turned friends into strangers and made strangers stay away. There were rare occasions when it didn't, but those were far and few in between.

She remembered one night when a woman had recognized her and had stopped by her table with a drink. She had smoky eyes and a pearl necklace.

"Violet?" She set her glass down on the table. "Violet Maslow? How long has it been?"

*Not long enough,* Violet thought. She sipped her gin and tonic.

"I'm Celeste," the woman continued. "Celeste Beauchemin."

"I know who you are," Violet said. "You dated my brother."

"You do remember! At first, I thought you forgot."

"How could I?"

"I don't know. I'm sure he had others."

"He did." Violet took a drink. "But I remember you."

Celeste paused, lifting her glass from the table. It was coldly-beaded and left a ring on the wood. "It's good to see you," she said.

Violet said nothing.

"Aren't you going to say it's good to see me, too?"

"I would, if it was."

"It isn't?"

Violet shrugged.

"Are you all right?"

"Sure," she said. "I'm all right."

"You don't sound all right."

"I'm fine."

"Well, all right," Celeste said. "I suppose you don't care how I am."

"How are you?" Violet asked.

"Fine, most of the time."

"And what about the rest of the time?"

"Blue. Black and blue."

"I know the feeling," Violet said. "The war makes everything gray..."

Celeste shook her head. "It's not that."

"No?"

"I don't think so."

"Then what is it?"

"My heart hurts," she said. "I feel broken."

"Why's that?"

She took a drink and heaved a sigh. "Where should I begin?"

"Why don't you start with my brother?"

"William was a darling. He ruined me..."

"Don't call him that. Nobody called him that. He went by Bill."

"I called him William, from time to time."

"I know, and he hated it."

"He never seemed to mind around me."

"I'm telling you he did."

"Hm. Maybe that's why he left me."

"No," Violet said. "He left you because of what you did. You slept around behind his back."

Celeste paused mid-sip and swallowed. "I—didn't think he knew."

"He did. I did, too."

She set her glass back down on the table. It was sweating. "I didn't realize."

"I figured as much."

"Violet," she said. "I'm very sorry."

"You could've told him."

"It was just a fling. I didn't think it meant anything."

"It meant a lot to him."

"I'm sorry," she said again. "The next time I see him, I'll tell him myself."

"You won't."

"I will—I swear I will."

"You won't get the chance," Violet said. "He's dead, Celeste. He died a year ago."

"What do you mean?"

"He was shot down overseas."

"Oh." Celeste looked down at her drink. "I didn't know he was drafted."

"He wasn't. He enlisted. My husband did, too."

"I'm very sorry."

"I'm sure you are."

"Really, I am."

"That doesn't make it any better."

Violet stared off toward the dresser with a bitter taste in her mouth. She couldn't recall how their conversation had ended that night, or how many other conversations they'd had. She did remember reading Celeste's obituary. She had died in the summer of '45.

She left the bedroom for the kitchen, feeling vaguely empty. It still smelled of coffee, and she poured herself a cup of what was left. She drank it in silence until Izzy came and found her. She sat at Violet's feet, looking up at her with her big brown eyes. There was comfort in her company.

When Violet finished her coffee, she decided to do some sweeping. She swept the kitchen first, then the living room, then the bathroom. Then she figured since she had swept the kitchen, it would be foolish not to clean it completely. She wiped down the table and the countertop, scrubbed the grates of the stove, and checked the expiration dates in the pantry. She washed all the dishes in the sink, watered the basil plant on the windowsill, and organized the contents of the cupboards and the refrigerator. Cleaning was a good distraction. She packed Greg's suitcase and Izzy's things late that afternoon. Izzy watched her, between naps.


Greg got home around four. He kissed her at the door and she could feel how tired he was.

"You had a long day."

He shrugged. "It wasn't too bad. It only dragged because there was somewhere else I wanted to be." He smiled at Izzy, who was sitting by their suitcases. "How's she been?"

"The same. She slept most of the day."

"I figured. She'll probably sleep most of the drive, too." He leaned down to pat her. "You girls ready?"

Violet nodded. "We're ready."

She helped Izzy down the front steps while Greg carried their suitcases out to the car. They let Izzy in the back, where she sat and rested her head between the driver and passenger seats. Violet got in next, then Greg. He started the engine, loosened his tie, and took a deep breath.

"You sure you're ready?" he said.

Violet met his gaze and answered with her eyes. "Are you?"

"I think so." He put the car in reverse and backed out of the driveway. "Home is home, after all..."

Izzy looked up at them, and Violet kissed her snout. *This is for you*, she thought. *For you and for Bill.*

They drove from Chestnut Street to Elm Street, which was stalled with traffic. Greg waited awhile before someone let him into the southbound lane, and they were off from there. The traffic dispersed outside of Camden, and they cruised down the coastal highway without delay. The land was a patchwork quilt of rolling hills and windswept fields, spread out beside the shimmering sea. Maine was boundlessly beautiful.

# 6

They hit traffic again in Bath, on the enormous bridge that stretched over the bay. Beneath them were the towering masts of the tall ships in the crowded marina. On the other side of the bridge, a portly fisherman in a yellow raincoat was selling lobsters. Violet waved to him as they passed. Nearby was a white wooden sign that welcomed them into town.

"*Bath—City of Ships,*" Greg read. "*Settled in 1781.* It's an old town, isn't it?"

"Older than Camden," Violet agreed. "But not quite as old as Portsmouth."

"How old is Portsmouth?"

"Old," she recalled. "I think it was settled around the same time as Hampton."

"When was that?"

"The 1630s, I think. Maybe even the 1620s."

"You have a damned good memory."

"It was home. It's hard to forget."

Greg readjusted his grip on the steering wheel. "It's strange to think we're going back. It feels a bit like we're headed into the past."

Violet patted Izzy as she slept. "In a way, we are," she said. "Only, Bill won't be there."

The traffic thinned beyond Bath and for an hour or so, they drove in silence. Route One was clear through Brunswick and Freeport, and even through much of Portland.

Greg cleared his throat. "I wonder how it'll feel to be back..."

"The same, I'm sure."

"Well, hopefully not as sad."

"No, but probably just as bitter." She recalled the emptiness of the morning. "As bitter as a strong cup of coffee..."

"Or a cool glass of Campari..."

"I like that better," she said. "Let's have one tonight."

"At Al Mare's," he said. "Tonight, and tomorrow night, too."

South of Portland, the drive was smooth and uninterrupted. They reached the New Hampshire border around seven, when the sky was burning gold, and crossed the bridge into Portsmouth. Below the bridge, on the banks of the Piscataqua River, was the Naval Shipyard. Beyond were the red brick buildings and the great white steeple of the old colonial city.

On the other side of the bridge, Route One became Daniel Street and led to the heart of downtown. Before they ended up in Market Square, Greg veered off to find them a hotel. There was an impressive-looking one on Bow Street, and he pulled the car up front. Its name was emblazoned across the awning that hung above its entrance: *The Hotel Piscataqua.* An international display of flags flanked the glass revolving door. A pair of straight-faced bellhops stood guard outside.

"I'll be damned," Greg said. "Portsmouth's far fancier than it used to be."

"Apparently," Violet said. She was watching the couples out in the courtyard. The men were striding about in three-piece suits while their wives glittered with confidence. There were no dogs to be seen.

Greg cut the engine. "Should we give it a try?"

Violet hesitated.

"What?"

"I don't know, Greg. They don't really seem like our type of crowd."

He swatted the air with his hand. "They don't have to be. We won't have anything to do with them. We'll have our room, and they'll have theirs."

"That's assuming they give us a room."

"They will. I'm sure they will."

Between them, Izzy stirred and blinked. Violet patted her head. "Well, hello, you sleepy girl..."

Greg unbuckled his seatbelt. "Should we take her out or leave her here?"

"I'll stay with her," Violet said. "You go in and see what they have."

He kissed her cheek and Izzy's snout. "All right."

He got out of the car and strolled across the courtyard, nodding at the couples as he went. Violet saw him pass through the revolving door and disappear into the hotel. He was inside for not more than ten minutes before he reemerged and came slouching back.

"To hell with that," he said, slamming the door. "Let's find somewhere else."

"What happened?"

He started the engine and pulled away from the curb. "We didn't get a room."

"Well, you don't say," Violet said. "How come?"

"The clerk was an ass," Greg said. "I told him we had a dog and he laughed in my face. Then he waved me along. Told me I was holding up the line." He shook his head. "Nice lobby, though. There was a mahogany desk and a crystal chandelier. I don't know when the hell Portsmouth got so goddamned fancy."

"It must've been while we were gone."

"I didn't think we had been away for *that* long."

"It's been five years, hasn't it?"

"Yeah, I guess it has."

They turned back onto Daniel Street, followed it to where it became Congress Street, and passed straight through Market Square.

Greg glanced at Violet from the steering wheel. "You can say it," he said.

"What?"

"Go on and say it—that you told me so."

She laughed. "You know I'm not one to do that."

"I know, but you were right. That wasn't our type of crowd."

"Honestly," she said, "I'm glad it wasn't. Those people seemed boring as hell."

They turned down Fleet Street and drove the length of it, passing a bank and a barbershop and an attorney-at-law. At the intersection with Court Street, Greg went left. They passed the fire station and made for the old, old houses of Strawberry Banke.

"Let's try here," he said, pulling in front of one. It was a two-story white colonial with patriotic buntings hanging below its windows. A handsome sign stood beside the brick pathway leading up to its door. *The Mariner's House,* it said.

They rolled the windows a quarter of the way down and left Izzy in the car. Inside The Mariner's House, it smelled of candlewax and clean linens. The front desk was at the end of a narrow hallway with a creaky floor. The clerk smiled at them as they approached. He had silver slicked-back hair and a broom handle mustache.

"Checking in?" he said.

Greg nodded. "If there's still vacancy."

"There is." He scanned the book before him and scratched his mustache. "How long will you be staying?"

"Two nights. We're headed back to Maine on Thursday."

"Wonderful. Your name?"

"Eastmor. Greg and Violet Eastmor."

He scribbled it down. "And it's just the two of you?"

"There's actually one more. She's waiting out in the car."

"Ah," the clerk said. "Then you'll want a room with two beds."

"One bed is fine," Greg said. "She sleeps on the floor, anyway."

The clerk looked up from his book. "Your child?"

"No. Our dog."

"Ah," he said again. "Your dog."

"She's very old and very well-behaved," Greg said. "She doesn't bark, she doesn't dig, and she knows not to go to the bathroom inside."

"Can you guarantee that?" the clerk asked.

"Absolutely. You'll hardly even know she's here."

"And she won't bother the other guests?"

"No. We can guarantee that, too."

The clerk set his pencil on the desk. "May I see her?"

"Of course."

He followed them out of the house and down the brick pathway to the curb. Inside the car, Izzy was sleeping.

The clerk peered in at her and chuckled. "Look at that—her whiskers are as white as mine."

"Just about," Greg agreed. "She's a very old girl."

"And you said she's well-behaved?"

"Extremely. She'll probably sleep most of the time."

"I don't blame her," the clerk said. "If I didn't have a hotel to run, I'd be doing that, too." He stepped away from the car. "Do you travel with her often?"

"As often as we can," Greg said.

"Do hotels normally take her?"

"Eventually. It takes some talking, but they usually come around."

The clerk laughed. "Then you must have this conversation all the time."

"We sure as hell do."

"But it's worth it," Violet said. "She's part of our family."

"I can see that. She clearly means a lot to you." He glanced at Greg, then at Violet. "Can you guarantee I won't regret it?"

They nodded.

"All right," he said. "But it'll cost you extra."

"Not a problem," Greg said.

The clerk scratched his mustache. "I haven't told you how much yet."

"Whatever it is, we'll pay it."

He glanced at them again, one after the other. "That dog is lucky to have you..."

"She knows it," Greg said.

Violet smiled. "And we're lucky to have her."

"Come on inside," the clerk said. "Let's get you a room."

# 7

It was a big room on the second floor with two windows that looked out over the street. The windows were partly open and the curtains were pulled back to let in the soft glow of the dusk. The pillows and bedspread were sea-blue, and the walls were the color of sand. Above the dresser hung a painting of a three-masted schooner.

The door to their bathroom was open, and Violet looked at herself in the mirror. Greg saw her looking and kissed her cheek.

"You look beautiful," he assured her.

"I look tired. You do, too."

Izzy wandered around the room, sniffing as she went. Finally, she settled on a spot at the base of the bed and collapsed with a sigh. She rested her head on her paws and gazed up at them.

"She's more tired than both of us," Greg observed. "What do you say we let her rest and go out on the town?"

"I say we try feeding her first." Violet opened her suitcase on the bed and took out the brown paper bag of Izzy's food. She stooped down with a palmful of pellets and held out her hand. Izzy ate them slowly, then sniffed around for more.

Greg found her bowl in Violet's suitcase and got it ready. He coated the food with water from the bathroom sink and set it down by Izzy's snout.

Violet straightened up and stood beside him. "She's eating slower than usual."

"She must be tired," Greg said.

They watched her finish her dinner, lick her chops, and rest her head on her paws once more. Violet took her bowl away.

"She's very tired."

"She always is." Greg leaned down to pat her. "Let's leave her here to rest."

"You don't think she'll get into trouble?"

"She's too old to get into trouble. Too tired and too old." He smiled. "She'll be fine."

They said their goodbyes and stepped out into the hall. Izzy's eyes were closed by the time Greg shut the door.

Outside The Mariner's House, night was falling steadily. The streetlights had flickered to life and the sidewalk was dancing with shadows. The houses and hedges were huddled together in the dark. They walked, hand-in-hand, to the corner of Court and Pleasant Street. Ahead was the old Portsmouth Custom House, now a bustling beatnik bar. Poets were drinking and discussing their work outside on the street-facing patio. There were cafés and restaurants all along Pleasant Street, their patron-packed tables shrouded in cigarette smoke and languid conversation. At the corner of Pleasant and State Street, Greg squeezed Violet's hand.

"Are you all right?" he asked. "You're quiet."

"I'm fine," she said. "You know how I get."

"You're worried about her."

She nodded.

"What are you afraid of?"

"I don't know. It's silly."

"Don't talk like that. What is it?"

"Well," she said. "I have this feeling she won't be there when we get back. I'm afraid she's going to leave us."

"Not tonight."

"Yes, tonight."

"Come on, Vi."

"I told you it was silly."

"It is," he said. "She wouldn't do that. Not here. Not tonight. She's too good of a girl."

"You talk about it like she can control it."

"Who says she can't? She's the only one who knows when she's ready."

"I've always hoped we'll be able to tell."

"I'm sure we'll be able to," Greg said. "But we don't have to talk about that now." The neon lettering of the sign for Al Mare's was a short distance away. "Let's have something to eat and something to drink and try our best to forget about it."

The terrace outside Al Mare's was crowded, and the host scanned the tables when they came up. "There's an hour wait inside," he told them. "But I can try to fit you in somewhere out here."

"Whatever you can manage," Greg said. "I didn't even think to make a reservation."

The host guided them to their seats and handed them each a menu. "Your waiter will be right along," he said—and sure enough, he was.

"Something to drink?" he asked them.

The man at the table next to them looked back. "Yes," he said. "We'll have another bottle of—"

"Robert," his wife said, and he stopped talking. She gestured to Greg and Violet, and he turned red. "So sorry," he said, turning back around.

The waiter blinked and repeated his question.

Greg laughed. "We'll both have Campari."

"How would you like it—neat, chilled, or in a spritz?"

"Neat, please."

"Certainly." He stepped back from the table. "I'll give you a moment to look over your menus."

"Thanks very much," Greg said, and the waiter turned to Robert and his wife. "Another bottle for you two?"

"Please," Robert said, still very red in the face.

The waiter checked the label, jotted the name down on his pad, and was gone.

Robert smiled sheepishly. "Sorry about that. I thought he was talking to me."

"It's no trouble," Greg said. "What was that wine you ordered?"

"It's a French red—a Côtes du Rhône. Beautiful stuff, if you'd like to have some."

"We know better than to finish another bottle," his wife added, smirking at her husband. "This one's already had too much."

"Oh, hush," Robert said. "Don't mind my wife. She gets this way when she's had a bit to drink."

"We both do," she said. "But that's beside the point." She smiled at them. "I'm Muriel. He's Robert. We've had a bottle of wine, so excuse us, *s'il vous plait.*"

Violet laughed. "It's a pleasure," she said. "I'm Violet. He's Greg."

They shook hands all around.

"Good to meet you," Robert said. "Nice place, isn't it?"

"Very nice," Greg said. "One of our favorites. We used to come here all the time."

"Why'd you stop?"

"The war, then the aftermath. We moved to Maine in '45."

"Ah," Robert said. "The war put a stop to a lot of things, didn't it?"

Muriel rubbed his arm. "I hardly smiled when you were away."

"It was hell for us, too," Violet said. "Greg was in Italy. So was my brother."

"Different parts of Italy," Greg said. "I was in Foggia. I'm not sure where he was. I was a crew chief on B-17s."

"The Flying Fortress? I'll be damned..."

"Yes, sir. Where did you serve?"

"France."

"No kidding."

Robert nodded. "Canadian Infantry."

"D-Day?"

"No, after." He shook his head. "I knew people who were there, though. What a time that was."

"A hell of a time," Greg said. "I'm glad I was in the air. I made it out all right. A lot of others didn't."

Violet stared down at the table.

"Here comes the waiter," Muriel said.

He was carrying a tray of drinks and a bottle of wine. "Two Camparis," he said, setting them before Greg and Violet. "And another bottle of Côtes du Rhône." He uncorked it ceremoniously, cradling the neck of the bottle with a white cloth napkin.

"Thank you, good sir," Robert said. "Would you bring us two empty glasses in case they want to try some?"

"Certainly." He turned to Greg and Violet, pen and pad ready. "Can I get you two anything?"

"I'll have the scampi," Greg said.

"That's what we had," Muriel cut in. "It was divine..."

The waiter glanced at her, then at Violet. "And for you?"

"Could I have the chicken cannelloni?"

He nodded and wrote it down. When he was gone, Robert nudged his wife. "Who's had too much to drink now?"

She rolled her eyes and held out her glass. "Pour a lady a drink, will you?"

He refilled their glasses and raised his own. "Cheers."

They all drank.

"How long are you in Portsmouth?" Violet asked.

"For the week," Robert said. "With the summer crowd gone, we figured it would be nice to get away."

"And it has been," Muriel said. "Portsmouth is a wonderful city."

"Is it just the two of you?"

"Oh, yes. People are always on us about having children, but they hardly know the time of day. Do you have any?"

Violet shook her head.

"Well," Greg started. "We do have her."

"Yes, but she's more of an old lady, if anything."

Muriel laughed. "Who's this?"

"Our old dog," Greg said. "We bring her everywhere we go."

"She's not here with you now," Robert observed.

"No," Violet said. "She's sleeping, back at the hotel. She's been very tired lately, so we figured we'd let her rest."

"We've never had a dog," Muriel said.

"We've never really had anything," Robert agreed. "Just ourselves." He grinned and took a drink. "But that's all right. She's more than enough for me to take care of."

Muriel rolled her eyes again. "Don't mind him," she said. "What kind of dog do you have?"

"She's a black Labrador retriever," Violet said. "She's gone white around her snout, but her eyes are young and bright."

"She sounds lovely," Muriel said. "We'd love to meet her before you leave."

"I'm sure we could arrange that."

"When do you go back to Maine?" Robert asked.

"Thursday afternoon," Greg said. "I have work on Friday morning."

"That's a drag. We go back on Sunday."

"Are you driving or flying?"

"Driving. I haven't flown since the war."

"You learned how to fly in the Infantry?"

"Learned, no. I was friends with a pilot in the Royal Air Force and he took me up, once or twice." He sipped his wine. "But you must've flown all the time. B-17s, didn't you say?"

"Yes," Greg said. "And biplanes, before that. I used to fly at an airfield about twenty minutes from here. That's where I learned. Violet's brother taught me."

"I'll be damned," Robert said. "Do you fly there much nowadays?"

"Not really, no. This is the first time we've been back here since the end of the war."

"What changed?"

Greg looked at Violet. "Everything. Nothing felt the same."

"I hear you," Robert said. "The day disappears with the dusk, and that's just the way it is. It's just one of those goddamned things."

Violet finished her Campari. It was bitter on her tongue.

Not long after, their food arrived. Everything looked and smelled delicious.

"You mind if we try some of your wine?" Greg asked. The waiter had brought them two extra glasses just in case.

"Absolutely." Robert handed him the bottle of Côtes du Rhône.

Greg filled their glasses halfway and handed it back. Robert topped off Muriel's glass, then emptied what was left of the bottle into his own. They toasted each other with a collective *clink*.

Violet closed her eyes as she drank. It really was beautiful wine, and it paired excellently with her chicken cannelloni. She ate and drank slowly, relishing the way the wine was now and then smoothed over by the spice notes of the sauce and the warm creaminess of the ricotta. Everything about it warmed her to the core. It felt good to be back at Al Mare's, and even better to be dining with friends.

Greg savored his scampi until the end, settling back in his chair. He looked very comfortable with his glass cradled in the palm of his hand. "You know what, Robert? You were right. This is damned good wine. Really excellent stuff."

"Isn't it?" Robert said. "What did I tell you? What did I tell them, Muriel?"

"You told them lots of things," Muriel said, tipping her glass back. "I can hardly remember all of them."

"I told them it was beautiful wine. Didn't I, Violet? It's simply beautiful."

"It is," she said. Under the wine, the night didn't feel so dark. "All of this is."

"All of this is," Robert repeated. "It absolutely is. Good food, good wine, and good company—that's all a person really needs."

"Cheers to that," Greg said.

Violet laughed. "Cheers to everything."

They drank until the wine was gone. Robert stretched and lit a cigarette. Muriel plucked one from the pack on the table and leaned into her husband's lighter. She took a puff, held it, and let it out. Robert smiled at her through the smoke. She noticed and smiled back.

Violet smiled at all of it. It was nice to smile—at everything, and at nothing at all. She glanced at Greg. He was smiling, too.

The waiter came up, cleared their plates away, and asked if they would have any dessert. Robert and Muriel said they weren't hungry. Greg and Violet said they weren't, either.

"Can I get you something else to drink?" the waiter asked.

Robert looked at Muriel, then at Greg and Violet. "What do you say—one more?"

"Only if we can get it," Greg said. "You paid for the Côtes du Rhône, so it's only fair."

"All right," Robert said. "What should we have?"

"Ever had Campari?"

"Yes, sir, but not since the war."

"What about you, Muriel?"

She shook her head. "Is it French?"

"Italian," the waiter said. "It's usually served as an aperitif."

"It's good at any time," Greg assured her. "It's bitter, but the better part of it tastes like oranges."

Muriel shrugged. "Let's have one. If I don't like it, someone else can drink it."

"All right."

"Four Camparis," the waiter said. "And both bills, too?"

"We'll get them," Robert said quickly.

"Robert," Violet said.

Muriel touched her hand. "Hush."

"You don't—" Greg started.

"We'll get them," he said firmly. "And that's the final word."

"Of course, sir." The waiter left the table.

Greg rubbed his forehead. "You didn't have to do that."

"Not at all," Violet said.

"We know," Muriel said. "We wanted to."

Robert tapped out his cigarette. "It's not often we come across people like you. You're damned good company."

"So are you," Greg said. "We'll get the bill next time—let's say, tomorrow night."

"Deal," Robert said.

The waiter returned with four glasses of Campari, and Robert signed the bill. Greg put down a tip. The waiter tucked the money into his apron and wished them a nice night. They sat with their drinks and talked awhile longer.

Muriel swirled the Campari around in her glass. She had lit another cigarette and was taking sips between puffs. "I can see why you two love this stuff," she said. "It's simply divine..."

"It makes me think of memories," Robert said. "Though of what, I'm not quite sure."

"That has to be a lie," Muriel said. "You remember everything."

"It's true." He marveled at his glass. "Usually, I do. But right now, my head's in the clouds and I don't feel so bad about it. What time should we all have dinner tomorrow?"

"Any time," Greg said. "What about six?"

"All right. Six, it is."

"Excellent—and tomorrow night, we'll get the bill."

"Thanks again," Violet said.

"Of course," Robert said. "This was a lovely time. You're both damned good company."

"Bring your dog tomorrow," Muriel said. "We'd love to meet her."

"We just might," Violet said. "It'll depend on how tired she is."

"If she's too tired, then let her sleep," Robert said. "Life is exhausting."

"She gets more than enough sleep. She's old, but I wish she wasn't so tired."

"Ah, well," he said. "We're all a bit tired, aren't we?"

They finished their Camparis in relative unison and, at length, stood up to leave. Violet took her time getting up. Her head was pleasantly swimming, and she clutched Greg's arm for support. He seemed a fair deal steadier than she was.

They stumbled over the chairs and off the terrace. It had cleared out significantly as the night had progressed. On the sidewalk, Greg and Robert shook hands.

"Till tomorrow?"

"Yes, sir."

"Goodnight, you two."

He and Muriel headed down State Street, while Greg and Violet crossed over onto Daniel Street. They followed the sidewalk down the hill to the pier beside the Memorial Bridge. The water of the harbor was a shimmering reflection of the starlit sky. Violet rested her arms on the railing, and Greg hugged her from behind. It was a beautiful night.

He kissed her and she sighed into his lips, vaguely lightheaded by the time he pulled away. He told her he loved her with his eyes and leaned in once more. His embrace was a gentle synonym.

"You're lovely," she said.

"You are," he whispered.

"Dinner was wonderful."

"It was," he said. "They're wonderful people."

She paused. "We could learn to be more like them."

"In what way?"

"They live in the present. We could do that, too."

"Tonight, I think we are."

"You think so?"

She felt him nod. "Tonight, we're not so bitter. We're a young couple in an old city, and we're having a wonderful time."

She raised her face to kiss him. "We certainly are."

# 8

The next morning, they walked down to one of the cafés on Pleasant Street and sat outside beneath a big umbrella. The tables of the terrace were contained by a makeshift wall of flower barrels, and the flowers were the color of the dawn and the dusk. Izzy sniffed them and sneezed. Greg chuckled. Violet patted her beneath the table.

They each ordered scrambled eggs, bacon, and wheat toast. It was a small and simple meal. Violet fed some of her eggs to Izzy, and Greg let her have a strip of bacon. She kissed their hands in return.

After they finished eating, they ordered a coffee and watched the traffic and took their time. They were the only ones out on the terrace, and the entire street was resonant with calm. The cars moved smoothly and easily down the road, their horns silent. It was a peaceful and promising morning.

Violet settled back in her chair. The coffee was bold and bitter, with a beautiful aroma. She drank it black, but she hadn't always. Growing up, she drank it with cream and a little bit of sugar. During the Depression, she stopped drinking it with cream because life was no longer rich. After Bill died, she stopped drinking it with sugar because life was no longer sweet. Life was, altogether, very bitter. Black coffee reminded her of that. She wondered if that was why her husband drank his coffee black, too.

"Greg?"

"Yes, Vi?"

"Has anyone ever asked you why you drink your coffee black?"

He thought for a moment, taking a sip from his cup. "I'm sure someone has, at one point or another."

"Have I?"

"I don't think so." He shrugged. "But I'll tell you, if you want to know."

"Will you?"

He shrugged again. "Sure. I just like the way it tastes."

"There isn't more to it?"

"I don't think so." He took another sip. "There might be, but I haven't really thought about it. I'm guessing you have?"

She nodded.

He smiled, intrigued. "Talk to me."

"Well," she said, "on the surface, I drink it black for the same reason you do."

"You like the way it tastes."

"I do—but for me, it's more than that. I like the way it reminds me, too."

"Reminds you of what?"

"Of how things are," she said. "Of the way life is."

Greg took a sip of coffee.

"It's bitter," she said.

"Yes."

"Life's bitter."

"No," he said. "Life's life and we're just bitter about it."

She sighed. "Sometimes I don't know why we still are. Shouldn't we be over it by now?"

"There's no 'should' or 'shouldn't' when it comes to grieving," Greg said. "I've learned that much, through the years."

"I don't know what I've learned," Violet said. "In the end, I guess I'm just bitter."

"I'm bitter, too, Vi. Don't feel so bad about it."

"I wish we weren't," she said, glancing beneath the table at Izzy. "I wish we were more like her."

"Yeah," he said. "I do, too."

She finished her coffee and set the empty cup on the table, feeling unpleasantly on edge. "You know what else I wish?"

"What?"

"I wish that coffee slowed you down instead of speeding you up. I feel like I'm buzzing right now."

He laughed. "I feel it, too. Want to go for a walk?"

Izzy perked up beneath the table.

"She does," Violet said.

"Do you?"

"Sure. Where should we go?"

"I don't know. Let's just walk."

"Sounds good to me."

They left the café and walked as though they were going to Al Mare's, passing it and pausing at the corner of State and Marcy Street. Directly ahead of them was Prescott Park, which overlooked the harbor and the Naval Shipyard. They followed the sidewalk alongside the wrought iron fence, passed the point where the fence ended, and went in. It was a lovely park, with long grassy aisles that led between the towering trees and blossoming flowerbeds. There were little placards in front of the flowerbeds that denoted their type and the names of their donors. Izzy lingered by the roses. She always seemed to like them the most.

They stopped at a bench to let her rest and gazed out across the water. The current was calm, but the Naval Shipyard was bustling and busy. It sounded like a construction site in the distance, and if Violet hadn't known any better, that's what she would've thought it was. There were massive submarines moored all about. Crewmen, in their white uniforms, were hard at work on their decks.

As busy as the Naval Shipyard currently was, she remembered how much busier it had been during the war. The navy had set up defense fortifications all along the New Hampshire coast, and Portsmouth had been the center of its operations. Scores of submarines had been launched from the harbor, and she'd even heard rumors that the captured crews of German U-boats had been held in the prison on-site. She asked Greg about the rumors, but he said he didn't know about them because he'd been away. She supposed it didn't matter now, since the war was over. They left the bench and walked back up the grassy lane.

In the middle of the park was a fountain, where a copper statue of Neptune was wrestling with a fish. The fish's mouth was open, and water was spewing out of it in a steady stream. A red ring of brick encircled the shallow pool below. Greg and Violet sat on it. Izzy sat nearby.

Violet's gaze wandered beneath the surface of the water. The base of the pool was studded with change that shimmered like scales—the results of countless wishes made and maybe granted. She rummaged around in her purse for a nickel or two to toss in.

"Here," she said, handing one to Greg. "Make a wish."

He balanced the coin on his thumbnail and flicked it into the water. It sank, with a glimmer, to the bottom.

"Aren't you going to make one, too?"

"Can't," she said. "I only had one nickel."

"Don't you have any other change?"

"Probably, but it's no use, anyway."

"Why's that?"

"Because the only things I'd wish for will never come true."

"No?"

"No," Violet said. "Bill's dead and there's nothing I can do to change that. Izzy's going to die and there's nothing I can do to change that, either."

Izzy looked up at her. There was love and light and a hint of reassurance in her old brown eyes. Violet managed a smile. "But you wished for something," she said.

"I did," Greg said.

"Good. I don't want to know what it was."

He raised an eyebrow. "You're not even a bit curious?"

"Oh, I'm extremely curious—but still, don't tell me."

"Why not?"

"Because," Violet said, "if you tell me, it won't come true."

"What does it matter, if it comes true or not?"

"Don't you want it to come true?"

Greg shrugged. "I don't know. I doubt it will, anyway."

She laughed and shook her head.

"What?"

"Listen to us," she said. "We sound so goddamned cynical."

"Well, we're bitter, aren't we?"

"I guess—but from the way we talk, you'd think nothing good ever happens to us."

He smirked. "You're right," he said. "We can be as bitter as we want, but life still goes our way sometimes."

"Only sometimes," she said. "My God, we're cynical..." She glanced at Izzy, who—even in her old age—appeared all the way optimistic. "We could learn a thing or two from her, don't you think?"

Greg nodded. "She's a smart girl, and she's already at peace with so many things."

They sat there by the fountain, observing her in silence.

"I wished that I would get to fly again," Greg said suddenly. "I know you said not to tell you, but like I said—I really doubt it'll come true."

Violet pursed her lips. "Hm."

"What?"

"Oh, nothing," she said. "I'm just thinking."

"About what?"

"We're going back to Hampton today, aren't we?"

"Only if we want to," he said. "Portsmouth is pretty nice."

"It is," she agreed. "But there isn't an airfield in Portsmouth."

"I don't know, Vi..." He met her gaze. "We haven't flown there in years."

"I know." She sighed. "But what else are we doing in Hampton besides giving it a try?"

# 9

They walked back to The Mariner's House to get the car and set out for Hampton around noon. Greg took the back way. It was a quiet trip. They drove from Portsmouth into Rye, and then into North Hampton. There, the road was a straightaway that led through a four-way intersection. They would cross into Hampton if they continued straight through, and Bill's old house would be on the right. They went left instead, toward the sea. Violet rolled her window down. The air was saline and solemn.

Along the coast, the road was bordered by blushing beach roses and sheltered by a long gravel embankment. Violet had stood atop that embankment more times than she could count, watching the waves curl and crash against the crestfallen shore. During the war, the view had brought her peace. When Bill died and it hurt to be in Hampton, the ocean had been a soothing friend. It was just as soothing now, with Greg home for good and Izzy still by her side.

She patted Izzy's head and offered Greg her hand. He squeezed it gently.

"I'm glad we went this way," she said.

"Me, too." His grasp was kind and comforting.

The road curved on toward Hampton. Izzy yawned, and Violet stroked her ears. "Wake up, sleepy girl..."

"There's a pull-off up ahead," Greg said. "Want to get out and stretch our legs?"

"Sure."

They parked by a gap in the gravel embankment and got out together. Violet opened the back door and took hold of Izzy's leash. She eased herself out of the car with a sigh, shaking off her exhaustion.

They walked down to the sand, where the tide was calm and contemplative. A flock of seagulls took flight as they went by. Izzy's pawprints marked their path across the shore.

After a short stroll beside the water, they made their way back to the car. From the pull-off, it was a quick drive into town. They picked up High Street by the Old Grist Mill and passed through the intersection known as Five Corners. The airfield, Violet remembered, would be on their left—before they reached the traffic light and Hampton's bustling downtown. It was a vast tract of land bisected by a dirt road that led to a row of nineteenth-century barns. The airplanes were housed inside. She grimaced as she thought about their pilots. The war had claimed Bill—and several others, too. She didn't know what had become of the rest of them. She and Greg had moved to Maine before they could really find out.

She gazed out the window, waiting for the dirt road to come up. The only thing she saw were houses—brand new houses that looked exactly alike. They were white and neat and modular, with TV antennas instead of chimneys. There were dozens of them, spaced only a few feet apart, on either side of High Street.

"I don't remember these," Greg said. "Do you?"

"No," she said. "Not at all."

They approached the dirt road.

"Hm," he said. "Looks like they paved it. It only took them fourteen years."

Violet pointed at the telephone pole on the street corner. "They named it, too." Affixed to the pole was a green sign with white lettering.

*MOULTON ROAD,* it said.

They turned onto it. There were new houses all around.

"I don't like this," she said.

He said nothing.

"Greg, something's not right. These weren't here before, either."

"It's all right," he said, narrowing his eyes at the road. "Don't worry…"

But as they came up to where the airfield was supposed to be, he fell silent. They parked in the clearing by its former entrance. Beyond was a desolate no man's land. The airfield, in its entirety, had been torn up. Giant mounds of dirt and sod marked the distances between gaping craters in the ground. There were no barns and no airplanes to be seen. The only explanation was a sign at the edge of the clearing.

"*Future Site of Morningside Drive,*" Greg read. He rubbed his face. "What the hell…"

Violet shivered. She patted Izzy, haunted by the impermanence of it all. "I hate this," she whispered. "Let's get out of here."

Greg looked on awhile longer, then tore his eyes away. He backed out of the clearing without another word.

On High Street, they stopped at the traffic light and went straight through. On their left was Hampton Academy, with its sweeping sports field and greenish copper cupola. Adjacent to it was Academy Ave, which led down to the fire station and the Lane Memorial Library. The trees lining Academy Ave were towering and taciturn, and the road and buildings looked very different in the shade.

Violet turned away. After a slight hill, there was a cemetery on the right.

Greg slowed the car. "Want to go in?"

"No." She sighed. "But we might as well."

They passed through the gate and perused the narrow lanes. The evergreens cast somber shadows over the rows and rows of headstones. Most of the old stones were overgrown with weeds. The new stones were in the back. Many of them were accompanied by miniature American flags.

Bill's stone was among them. There had been no body for them to bury, so they had laid down a memorial tablet instead.

Greg parked alongside it and they all got out. Izzy sniffed at the grass and then at the tablet before settling down at their feet. The three of them stood there in silence, staring at the ground:

WILLIAM T. MASLOW

CPL USAAF

DEC. 4 1912 † APR. 25 1944

Violet tried not to cry. She told herself she wouldn't, but the numbness was too much. Her brother was dead and their airfield was gone. She sank to her knees and wrapped Izzy in a hug. Greg held them both.

They said nothing. She felt next to nothing. It was all empty. It was all gone.

The shadows of the trees were long and lamenting.

# 10

Outside the cemetery, they crossed the street and parked along Academy Ave. The trees loomed over the sidewalk and it was lonely without the sun. There was an old bronze bell out in front of Hampton Academy.

Violet pointed at it. "Remember where that came from?"

Greg thought for a moment. "I think they took it from the first academy," he said. "It was up in the cupola for quite some time. I don't know why they didn't put it up in the new one."

"I don't know, either." Violet considered the school's brick façade. "The first academy looked like a church. This one's quite a bit different."

"It was white, wasn't it? I know it was made of wood. It splintered easily when they tore it down."

"It did," she said, shivering in the shade. "I wish we hadn't watched."

He held her hand. "It was definitely strange. When was that—'40 or '41?"

"When was Pearl Harbor?"

"December of '41."

"Then it was in '40," she said. "Pearl Harbor hadn't happened yet."

"It was strange to watch," Greg said.

"I hated it."

"I can tell."

She sighed. "It's hard seeing things change."

"No kidding," he said. "At least the trees are somewhat the same. They're older and taller, but that's about it."

They walked on beneath them. Izzy trotted over their shadows.

"You and I aren't too different, either," he continued. "We were sweethearts then, and we're sweethearts now. The rest of it doesn't really matter."

She squeezed his hand. "We do all right together, don't we?"

"I think so." He squeezed hers back. "We've weathered the world for this long..."

They paused on the sidewalk to let Izzy catch her breath, then kept going. Hampton Academy was soon behind them.

"Did Bill ever have a sweetheart?" Greg asked.

"You'd know as much as I would," Violet said.

"But I don't."

"Neither do I."

"Oh, come on," Greg said. "He was your brother."

She shrugged. "We never really talked about it."

"Still," he said. "You would've noticed."

"He dated a few girls," she said. "But they hardly ever stuck around. He usually always ended up alone."

"That's a damned shame. He was a good guy. It would've been nice to see him happy."

"He was happy."

"I meant, with a girl."

"He didn't need a girl. He loved his dog."

They smiled down at Izzy. She looked back at them, wagging her tail.

"He loved his airplanes, too," Greg said. "I'll always remember that."

They neared the fire station and the Lane Memorial Library. Both were sepia in the shade.

"I miss my planes," he mused. "I like what I do, but it's nothing like flying. That was a fine chapter. A damned good time." He sighed. "But it's over now. Our airfield is gone."

They rounded the corner of Academy Ave and Winnacunnet Road. In the lot beside the fire station, they stopped short. Izzy sat solemnly between them.

Greg stared. "The hell happened to the town hall?"

The original, with its grand Victorian clocktower, had vanished. An ugly white office building now stood in its place.

"I guess they built a new one," Violet said.

"What was wrong with the first?"

"I don't know," she said. "Maybe it burned down."

"Come on, Vi..."

"It could've."

"There's no way," he said. "The fire station's right next door."

"That doesn't mean anything."

"It ought to."

She shrugged. "Why don't we go into the new one and ask?"

"That's not the point." He shook his head. "We've been away for five years, Vi. That's not that long of a time."

"I guess it was long enough," she said.

"Yeah," he said. "I guess it was."

They continued down Winnacunnet Road, still very much in the shade. The sidewalk stopped at the spot where Mill Road came in on the left, and they crossed the triangular patch of grass to regain it once more. Beyond were some of the oldest houses in town, settled in the shadows of the elms and evergreens. Some had barns and others had carriage houses, and their back-yards were fields bounded by lengths of split-rail fence. Nearby were the hallowed headstones of the Pine Grove Cemetery, where Hampton's earliest residents had been laid to rest.

Greg and Violet slowed their pace. The other end of Moulton Road was just ahead. When they reached it, Izzy sniffed the base of the telephone pole that bore the green and white sign. It stood out among the trees, an awkward marker of misplaced modernity.

Violet shook her head. Behind them were homes that had been standing for at least a century—but there was no guarantee that they would stand for a century longer. All that was good would in time be replaced with something gaudy. The fate of their airfield had showed her that.

She caught a glimpse of it through a gap in the houses on Moulton Road. It was nothing more now than a construction zone, an unfortunate casualty of what was new and neat and modular.

Greg followed her gaze. "I still can't believe it."

"I don't want to," she said.

Izzy finished sniffing around the telephone pole and returned to their side, ready to move on. Greg squeezed Violet's hand.

They took one last look at everything, then turned and walked back to the car.

They drove back to Portsmouth the same way they came. The road was downcast up the coast. The sea was slate-colored. The clouds were steely and gray.

"You know," Violet said. "They could've at least told us it was going to happen."

"Who?"

"I don't know," she said. "Anybody. If we had known the town was going to change, then maybe we wouldn't have stayed away so long. Maybe we would've come back sooner."

"Maybe," Greg said. "But then again, maybe not. It's near-impossible to say."

"Yeah, well, it would've been nice to know. We could've come back before they tore it all up. We could've said a proper goodbye."

"That would've been nice. We don't know a hell of a lot about proper goodbyes."

"We don't."

"I wish we did."

"Me, too, Greg."

"You know what else I wish?"

"What?"

"That we weren't so bitter about it."

"What's wrong with being bitter?" she said. "It beats being sad."

"I guess—but it's not much better."

The gravel embankment gradually receded as they crossed into Rye. The waves were sad and sullen, and the surf was swirling with melancholy.

Violet sighed. "I'm sorry you didn't get to fly again."

"It's all right, Vi."

"Are there other airfields around? Maybe there's somewhere else we could go."

He shook his head. "It wouldn't make any difference. Ours is gone. The others don't matter to me."

"They don't matter to me, either," she admitted. "I just know you wanted to fly."

"I'm not so keen on it anymore. It wouldn't be the way it was."

"Nothing's the way it was," Violet said. "Everything's different now."

"I know. I still hoped it wouldn't be."

"Me, too."

"But you know, I guess that's not a bad thing."

"You don't think so?"

"No. It just goes to show we're hopeful."

"What good does that do us?"

"I don't know." He glanced at her from the steering wheel. "It feels damned better than being bitter, if you ask me."

# 11

When they got back to Portsmouth, they stopped for coffee in Market Square. Violet drank hers slowly, settling into its bitterness. They sat without speaking at a table outside, watching the cars and people go by. Nobody seemed to be in much of a hurry. The traffic lagged and lingered a bit, then moved on.

Violet sighed. The tall brick buildings of the square were red and reticent against the sky. The coffee was black and her mind was gray. She gazed up at the white steeple of the Old North Church. The minute hand of its clock sank to half past two.

She observed Izzy beneath the table. Her head was resting on her paws. "Do you think she recognized it today?" she asked Greg.

"Hampton?"

"The airfield."

He took a long sip of coffee. "Probably not. There wasn't much for her to recognize."

She leaned down to pat her. "That's what I figured. Her home hardly feels like home anymore."

"It's very different," Greg agreed. "But at least she's at peace with it."

"She is, but we're not."

He said nothing.

She surveyed the square. "Maybe we should've stayed a little longer. We didn't even give her a chance to recognize it."

"It wouldn't have mattered, Vi."

"I guess not." She swallowed some coffee. "I just wish she got to see it the way it was."

"She's at peace with it," Greg said. "You know she is."

"I know," she said. "I just feel so bad."

"About what?"

"This trip. It was supposed to be for her."

"It still is."

"I guess."

"What do you mean, 'you guess?'"

"I don't know," she said. "Everything's so different now. She doesn't even know she's home."

"Hey," Greg said, and he squeezed her hand. "She absolutely does. She knows she's happy, and she knows she's here with us."

He tapped Izzy's tail with his foot. She looked back at them with love in her old brown eyes.

"See?"

Violet managed a smile. Izzy lowered her head to her paws once more.

"So," Greg said. He sipped his coffee and rested his cup on his knee. "Tell me—what do you remember about the airfield?"

"Oh, all sorts of things."

"Like what?"

"I don't know," she said. "I remember all sorts of things."

"Tell me one of them."

"All right—but only if you do, too."

"Deal."

She closed her eyes. "I remember the way the hangars smelled."

She heard him take a drink. "Talk to me."

"They smelled like engine oil and gasoline and old newspapers. I think they smelled a bit like hay, too, but that might be in my head."

"Why's that?"

She opened her eyes. "Because the hangars were barns long before they were hangars, but that was years and years ago. The airfield had been around for a decade when we started flying there. There's no reason why they would've still smelled like hay."

"They could've smelled like hay," Greg said. "The planes tracked grass in from the field all the time. Some probably ended up inside and dried out. It probably stayed there for a while. We hardly ever swept the floors."

"I guess that would explain it," Violet said. She contemplated a flock of pigeons that had congregated out in the square. "What's something you remember?"

"Hm." He gazed off in thought, watching the pigeons. "All right, here's something..."

"Let me hear it."

"What do you remember about the statue of St. Anthony?"

"The little one, outside Bill's hangar?"

"Yeah—the one without a head."

"I remember it." She laughed. "I don't know why he kept that thing."

"I don't know, either. I think he thought it was good luck."

"It was something," she said. "That's for sure."

Greg chuckled. "I always thought it was kind of funny. The patron saint of finding things had gone and lost his head..." He stretched in his chair. "What do you think happened to it?"

"The statue, or its head?"

"The statue. Didn't Bill say he found it without a head?"

She nodded. "He got it that way from a yard sale, I think."

"What do you think happened to it?"

"Oh, I'm sure it's long gone. They probably threw it out when they tore down the hangars—along with everything else."

"Probably." Greg sighed. "I'm sure they sold the planes for scrap, too."

"I'm sure," she said. "And now, it's gone. Everything we knew is gone."

They sat watching the pigeons in the square.

"What do you remember about flying?" she asked.

"Everything," he said.

"Do you remember our last flight?"

"Absolutely. Do you?"

She nodded. "It wasn't long after you got back from Italy."

"You're right," he said. "In the fall of '45. Before we sold the house and moved to Maine."

"I'll never forget it," she said. "It was a wonderful time."

"There were a couple of us there," Greg recalled. "Not nearly as many as before the war, but the ones that came back. You remember Russ?"

"Of course," she said. "Smitty. He was in the Pacific, wasn't he?"

"I think so."

"Where did he end up?"

"I think he moved down to Florida. He married that girl from Panama City. I don't know what he's doing for work. He might even have kids."

"He was a good one," Violet said. "He stayed with Izzy while we were up in the air."

"That's right." Greg grinned. "Covered her ears while we took off, too."

"I remember that." She set her coffee down on the table. "That was a fun time."

"It was." He set his coffee beside hers. "Did you fly at all before I got back?"

"Not once," she said.

"Really?"

"Yeah. Ours was the last flight I took since before you left."

"I'm surprised."

She shrugged. "There was no one to fly with. You and Bill and the others were gone. The airfield was all but deserted."

"You mean there was no one flying there at all?"

"No. There was hardly anybody. Haven't I told you that?"

"You've mentioned it was quiet, but I didn't realize it was dead." He sighed. "No wonder why the town put it up for sale."

"They kept it maintained," Violet said. "There was always someone around to cut the grass. But it was still pretty dead. The days before the war were definitely the best."

"What else do you remember?" Greg asked.

"About our flight?"

"Yeah."

She thought for a moment. "I remember the view," she said. "It was lonely. Beautiful, but lonely."

"Not much had changed," Greg said. "Hampton's always been that way."

"No, but still. I liked it more before the war."

"At least it didn't look too different. The farms were the same and the fields were the same, and the ocean was the same, too."

Violet winced. "I'm sure it looks worse nowadays, with all those new houses and neighborhoods."

"Probably." Greg drank some coffee. "The peace of the old days is gone."

"Do you think we'll ever get it back?"

"Not unless we remember. Our memories are all we have."

"I don't have too many," she said. "I feel like I should, but I don't."

"Not even of Bill?"

She sighed and shook her head. "It hurts too much, Greg. I know I have them, but I've gotten used to letting them be. I haven't forgotten them, either. I'm just too numb to remember. The past six years haven't made a difference. It still feels like too soon."

"I get it," he said.

"You do?"

He nodded. "That's how I am about the war. We both know I was there, but it feels much better not to talk about it."

"It's numbing," Violet said. "All of it is."

Again, Greg nodded. "Thank God it's over. I'd be happy if it never happened again."

"It won't," she said. "There's nothing left to fight about."

"I'm sure something else will come up."

She considered her coffee. "Maybe, but not for a while. Hitler and the others are dead."

"Sure," Greg said. "But now the Soviets are on the rise. Years from now, they'll get greedy. It'll happen all over again."

"I hope not," Violet said.

Greg finished his coffee. "Me, too."

Across the square, the bells of the Old North Church rang out three times. Izzy looked up at the sound.

"What do you think?" Greg said. "Should we head back?"

Violet stretched and stood up from the table. Her sunhat felt heavy on her head.

They walked back to the car. Greg had parked by the curb in front of the café. Inside, it was hot. Greg started the engine, and Violet rolled the windows down for Izzy. They waited for the traffic to clear, then backed out onto Congress Street. The jazz was blue on the radio.

# 12

The Mariner's House was dim and comfortable when they got in. They closed the curtains in their room but kept the windows partly open for the breeze. Izzy curled up on the floor, closing her eyes with a sigh. Greg and Violet watched her from the bed. Their eyes were heavy, too.

They lay, immersed in each other, atop the covers. The breeze was calm and comforting. The sounds of the city were soft and sincere. The day had been hell, but none of it mattered. Very soon, they were asleep.

They awoke to the distant bells of the Old North Church. Violet checked Greg's watch.

He yawned. "What time is it?"

"Five."

"It feels like nine."

She kissed him sleepily. "What time are we meeting Robert and Muriel?"

"Six, wasn't it?"

"I don't remember."

"I think it was six." He stretched and sat up. "It definitely was."

"Are you hungry?"

"A little. Are you?"

"Not really, but I could go for a drink."

Greg yawned. "After today, so could I."

She glanced at Izzy from the bed. "Are you awake, sleepy girl?"

Izzy grunted and stirred.

"She is now," Greg said.

Violet heard her come over to the bed and felt her nose against her hand. "Let's feed her before we go."

Greg got her food ready and set her bowl on the floor. Izzy ate slowly. When she was finished, she settled down for another nap.

Violet kissed Izzy's snout. "You be good while we're gone..."

"She will be," Greg assured her.

They walked to Al Mare's a different way—down to the corner of Court and Atkinson Street, then up Atkinson and onto State Street. When they arrived, the terrace was mostly empty. The evening was very young.

"Good to see you again," the host said. "Just two tonight?"

"We're actually expecting two more," Greg said. "But they won't be here for another hour or so. Could we hold a table outside?"

The host nodded. "Your names?"

"Greg and Violet Eastmor."

He scribbled them down in his book. "You're all set. In the meantime, you're welcome to have a drink at the bar."

"Thanks," Greg said. "I think we will."

Inside, the lights were low and a jazz trio was set up in the corner. A small crowd was spread out among the tables, but there was hardly anyone at the bar. Greg and Violet ordered vermouth. It was cool and melancholic. As they touched glasses, the trio played a pensive rendition of "Every Time We Say Goodbye."

Violet remembered the way it went. She sighed. "How many times have we said goodbye?"

"Too many," Greg said. He took a drink. "And you know what? I'd be all right if I never had to say it again."

"It's never easy."

"No, it usually isn't. It's hardly ever our choice."

"But we've said it a lot," she said. "To Bill, to the airfield, to Hampton. To the home we knew and the way things were. It's all gone now. It's all changed."

Greg nodded. "All of it."

Violet stared into her glass. The vermouth was honey-colored and tinged with heartache. The trio started in on another song. She didn't recognize it, but she was too numb to care.

"Here's to you," Greg said.

She leaned over and kissed his cheek. "Cheers."

They sat listening to the jazz for quite some time. It was moody and meditative, and in-tune with every moment. It solaced their sadness and spoke to their cynicism. Each note was a stanza of sonic poetry. It was even better with the vermouth. They had another before a waiter came up with Robert and Muriel in tow.

"Hello, you two," Robert said. Muriel waved her cigarette.

"Hello, hello," Greg said. Violet raised her glass.

The waiter gestured back toward the door. "Your table is ready, if you'll follow me."

They went with him out to the terrace and sat at a table beneath a big umbrella. He asked what they would have to drink.

"Water, for us," Greg said. "We've already had a couple."

Robert laughed. "You didn't tell us you were getting a head start. What've you had?"

"A bad day," Violet said.

Muriel rubbed her arm. "He meant, to drink."

"Vermouth," Greg said.

Robert addressed the waiter. "We'll have vermouth, to start."

"Of course, sir."

"And afterward, a bottle of cava."

"With four glasses?"

"Please."

The waiter hurried away. Robert turned his gaze to Greg and Violet. "Sorry to hear about your day…"

"It's all right," Greg said. "It's over now, anyway. How was yours?"

"It was nice. We woke up late, had breakfast around lunch, and walked around the city." He glanced at his wife. "What else did we do, Muriel?"

She took a puff from her cigarette. "We went to that art gallery on Penhallow Street."

"How was that?" Violet said.

"Simply divine. It was all local art with so much character. So many talented people call Portsmouth home."

"After that, we went out to Peirce Island," Robert said. "We sat on a bench and fed the ducks, and looked out over the water. It was a peaceful time."

"Peirce Island's wonderful," Greg said. "We went to Prescott Park this morning."

Muriel smiled. "The flowers are beautiful this time of year. Isn't it a shame they don't last forever?"

"It's sad," Violet said. "There's so much comfort in the roses."

The waiter returned with menus and drinks. They thanked him and he was gone.

Robert sipped his vermouth. "I hate to say it, but I'm not very hungry tonight."

"We had a late breakfast," Muriel reminded him. "And an even later lunch."

"I'm not that hungry, either," Violet said. She had a glass of water and poured herself some more from the jug on the table. "When he comes back, I'll probably have something else to drink."

"Why don't we order some bread?" Greg said. "They have excellent focaccia. I remember that from before the war."

"I trust your memory and your judgement." Robert grinned. "You said last night you used to come here all the time."

"We did," Violet said. "We used to live in Hampton, about twenty minutes from here. My brother had a place there. He and Greg used to fly at the airfield."

"Back when there was an airfield to fly at," Greg said.

Robert frowned. "What do you mean?"

"It's gone," Violet said. "We found out today. They've torn it all up to make room for a new neighborhood."

"Morningside Drive," Greg recalled. "The latest development in suburbia."

Muriel put out her cigarette. "What an odd name for a neighborhood."

"I think it's sort of symbolic," Robert said.

"How so?"

"Well," he said. "The day disappears with the dusk, and morning's the only thing to look forward to. To hell with the night."

Violet surveyed the terrace. The sun was sinking in the sky. She caught the waiter as he was going by. "Could we have a loaf of focaccia?" she asked.

"Of course."

"And that bottle of cava," Robert put in. "Thanks very much."

The waiter nodded and disappeared back inside.

Violet nudged Greg. "What's cava?"

"Sparkling wine, I think."

"Spanish champagne," Robert said. "It's beautiful stuff."

"We drink it all the time," Muriel added. "It's our Campari."

"It sounds nice," Violet said. "But I don't know what we're celebrating."

Robert toasted Muriel, and they finished their vermouth. "Champagne is for celebrating," he said. "Cava is for acknowledging. Campari, it seems, is for thinking."

"It is," Greg said. "It's a very contemplative drink."

"What are we acknowledging?" Violet asked.

"Whatever you'd like." Robert shrugged. "The end of the war, the end of an era—maybe the end of a really bad day."

"I'll drink to that," Greg said, refilling his glass of water.

Violet sighed. It was a difficult thing, to acknowledge the end.

Muriel touched her arm. "Did you at least get to visit your brother?"

Greg grimaced, and Robert saw. "I know that look," he said.

Muriel glanced at them, then back at Violet. Her voice was all at once soft and rueful. "Violet," she said. "I'm so sorry."

"It's all right," Violet said. "He died during the war. His plane was shot down over Italy."

"I'm sorry to hear it," Robert said.

"It's all right. It's been years."

"That doesn't matter," Muriel said. "It's hell. We know it is. We've lost people, too."

"It sounds like we all have," Greg said.

"Yes, well—misery loves company, doesn't it?"

"It sure as hell does."

Robert contemplated his empty glass. "Now I understand why you moved away."

Violet nodded. "It was too lonely—too painful. Everything was different. Nothing felt the same."

"But you came back," Robert said. "Why?"

At first, she didn't have an answer. Then she remembered Izzy back at The Mariner's House and sighed. "Our dog," she said. "We figured we'd take her back home."

"It was the kindest thing we could do," Greg said. "She was everything to Violet's brother, and she's been everything to us."

"She's gotten old," Violet said. "Now seemed like the best time." She stared at the water jug on the table. It was glittering in the sunset. "I just wish her home was the way it was before the war. It's barely recognizable now. It feels like a slap in the face."

"I'm sure it means just as much to her," Muriel said.

"I hope so."

"It does," Greg said. "She's seen it for what it is, and for what it's been. She's at peace with all of it."

"But we're not," Violet said.

"I don't know if anyone is." Robert moved the jug aside for the waiter. "It's just one of those goddamned things."

The waiter set the focaccia bread down on the table. It was round and speckled with rosemary and sea salt. He brought them four stemmed glasses and the bottle of cava in a bucket of ice.

"We'll open it ourselves," Robert said.

"Very good, sir."

"And when the time comes," Greg said. "We'll get the bill."

"Of course." The waiter stepped back from the table. "Enjoy."

"Damned kind of you," Robert said.

"Don't mention it. You got it last night, after all."

They sliced the loaf into fourths and each took a piece. It was still warm. Violet dipped hers into the bowl of seasoned olive oil. The taste brought her back to better, less bitter days.

Robert lifted the cava from the bucket of ice. "Anyone for a drink?"

Muriel patted his hand. "Let's all have one," she said.

He unwrapped the foil from the top of the bottle and loosened the cork carefully. The *pop* was muffled, and there wasn't much froth. He poured them each a glass, going back and topping them all off until the bottle was empty. They toasted and drank.

Violet smiled. The cava was cold and dry and vaguely autumnal. It felt good to be sitting out on the terrace, drinking in the dusk in the company of friends. They settled back in their chairs, listening to the traffic and the tableside conversations and the cool, constant breath of the street. The cava quieted everything. All in all, things weren't so bad.

"What time are you going back to Maine tomorrow?" Robert asked.

"We're not sure yet," Greg said. "Probably sometime in the afternoon."

"Come by and see us before you leave," Muriel said. "We'd love to meet your dog…"

"Where are you staying?"

"At a hotel on Bow Street. I forget the name." She dug around in her purse and took out a pen and an old receipt. Robert wrote out the address.

"We'll come by," Greg said, tucking it in his pocket.

"Divine," Muriel said. "We can't wait to meet her."

"Only bring her by if she's not sleeping," Robert said. "Don't wake her up on our account."

"She gets plenty of rest," Violet said. "I'm sure she'll be awake."

"Excellent," he said. "She sounds like a lovely dog."

"She is. We're very lucky to have her."

"Clearly, she's very lucky to have you, too."

The waiter brought the bill and Greg paid it. Robert put down a tip. They finished their cava slowly, in relative silence.

When her glass was empty, Violet looked around. Greg was handsome and thoughtful. Robert and Muriel were benevolent and warm.

Greg saw her thinking. "What's on your mind?"

"Oh, everything."

"Good or bad?"

"Both," she said. "I'm happy to be here. I mean that, in every sense of the word."

"We're happy to be here, too," Muriel said. "It's been a lovely time."

"It really has been. You're wonderful people. You really are."

Robert studied his cava with brooding eyes. "We're all wonderful people," he said. "Damned shame we've lost some even better ones."

# 13

Greg and Violet spent the night with the window open, lulled to sleep by the swaying breeze and the soft sounds of the street. At daybreak, they made love in the nectarine glow of the sunrise, lounging for a while in the smiling aftermath. They fell back asleep and got up a couple of hours later. Izzy slept through both of their showers.

Violet, freshly dressed, patted her awake. "Good morning, sleepy girl..."

Izzy opened her eyes and yawned. With some difficulty, she got to her feet, stretching and shaking off her grogginess.

Greg scratched her behind the ears and fastened her leash to her collar. "I can take her out, if you want."

"Let's both take her out," Violet said. "Then we'll get something to eat."

"What about her?"

"We'll get her something, too."

They shut the door behind them and stepped out into the hall. All of the other rooms had "Do Not Disturb" signs affixed to their doors. They crept down the hall and down the staircase, passing no one. There was jazz playing quietly on the radio behind the front desk. The old clerk waved at them as they went by.

After Izzy did her business, they set off down Court Street in the direction of downtown. The cafés along Pleasant Street were crowded, so they walked on and had breakfast at a coffeeshop in Market Square. Their table faced the athenaeum and the towering white steeple of the Old North Church. It was a calm and quiet morning, and there were pigeons pecking about in the square. There weren't enough people out on the street to scare them away, and there was comfort in their company. Izzy watched them with mild interest. Violet stroked her head.

They ordered coffee and poached eggs on toast, and a plate of scrambled eggs for Izzy. Violet made crumbs from the crust of her toast and scattered them beyond the table. Before long, the pigeons came. Their cooing was quaint over the low hum of the traffic.

"Look at them go," Greg said.

Violet wiped her hands on her dress. "I like them," she said. "They have pretty voices."

"They do," he said. "They remind me of mourning doves."

Violet sipped her coffee. "So do we."

He laughed. "How so?"

"We've been mourning for a long time, haven't we?"

"We sure as hell have."

"It's exhausting," she said.

"It is."

"And there's hardly any peace in it."

"Hardly any at all."

They both drank. The coffee was good and strong.

"There's hardly any peace in it," Greg said. "But you know what?"

"What?"

"I'm sure there's peace in what comes after."

She raised an eyebrow. "You think so?"

"Sure. Nothing stays bad forever."

"What makes you say that?"

"Well, the war's over. There was a time when I didn't think that would ever end."

"I had a hard time believing it would, too."

"But it did," he said. "We lost a hell of a lot, but an ending came—even if it wasn't always in sight."

"That was a good ending, though," Violet said. "Good endings aren't hard to accept. Bad ones almost certainly are." She drank some coffee, considering the pigeons in the square. "I wish the good things in life lasted forever."

"I do, too—but they don't. It would do us some good to acknowledge that."

"Don't we already?"

"Not enough."

She stared down at Izzy. "Sometimes, I'm afraid to."

"I know, Vi. So am I."

She shook her head. "God only knows why."

"We probably know why, too."

"I don't."

"I might."

"All right," she said. "Why do you think we're afraid?"

He thought for a moment. "Well, if we accept the end, maybe that means we'll start forgetting."

She shook her head. "We'll never forget."

"No, but I think we're afraid we will. I think we're afraid of losing a part of what made Bill and Izzy so special to us. I think we're afraid of what it means to move on."

"I think you're right," she said quietly. "I don't like thinking about what it means to move on."

Greg finished his coffee and set his cup on the table. "I don't think it has to mean forgetting."

"You don't?"

"No. I don't think we have to forget a thing."

"Then how do we move on?"

"We raise our glasses to the world and acknowledge that it's changed. We realize that, somewhere along the line, we changed, too. We sit back and drink it in and accept it. It's not easy, but it's what we ought to do."

Violet contemplated her coffee, letting his words sink in. "Where'd you learn that?" she asked.

He looked down at Izzy, and she looked up at them. The sun was smiling in her eyes.

"She's accepted the end, Vi. She's found peace with it. If we tried, I think we could, too."

She hesitated. "It won't be easy."

"No, and I'm sure it'll take time. But listen—we ought to try it."

Violet took a deep breath. "Together?"

"Together," he said. "Always."

She smiled at him, then down at Izzy. "I guess she has taught us something, after all these years."

Greg patted her fondly. "She certainly has."

Across the square, the bells of the Old North Church rang out the time.

"Nine o'clock," Violet said. "Do you think Robert and Muriel are still sleeping?"

Greg shrugged. "Only one way to find out."

They stood and kissed and crossed the street. Izzy wagged her tail as the pigeons took flight.

They headed up Market Street away from the square, pausing now and then so that Izzy could catch her breath. They passed the dark windows of the unopened restaurants and smiled at the people sitting outside at the coffeeshops and cafés. On the corner of Market and Bow Street, Greg pulled out the address of Robert and Muriel's hotel.

"Ha," he said. "I'll be damned..."

"What?"

He showed her the scrap of paper. "Take a look at where they're staying."

She glanced at it and winced. "Didn't we go there before The Mariner's House?"

"We sure as hell did."

"And they laughed at you when you told them about Izzy?"

"That's right."

She made a face. "Why the hell are they staying there?"

"They must have gotten a room."

"Still," Violet said. "That's not their crowd."

"It's not," Greg agreed. "But it is a nice place."

They took their time getting to the hotel. Bow Street led up a hill to the five brick stories of the St. John's Chapel, giving way to its cemetery and sloping down to meet the bars and businesses on the other side. It rounded a bend and curved past the grand façade of the Hotel Piscataqua. Greg and Violet stopped in the courtyard out front.

The bellhops eyed them from either side of the glass revolving door. Izzy perked up when she noticed them, and Violet held tight to her leash.

"I don't think they'll let us in, Greg."

"The hell they won't. Let's at least try."

They approached the door. The bellhops exchanged glances.

"Good morning," Greg said, grinning at them. "Beautiful day, isn't it?"

One of the bellhops stepped in front of the door. The other narrowed his eyes.

"Excuse us," Greg said, looking past them. "We're just going in to visit some friends."

"Not with that dog, you're not."

"Oh, come on. She's very well-behaved."

"That's beside the point," the straight-faced bellhop said. "No dogs are allowed inside."

"Not even for a minute? Our friends should be right down."

The straight-faced bellhop shook his head. "Not even for a minute. It's hotel policy."

Izzy looked up at them, wagging her tail. The bellhop blocking the door cracked a smile. "That's one happy dog," he remarked.

"Very happy," Greg said. "She'd be even happier if she could go inside."

The straight-faced bellhop shook his head as his partner shuffled out of the way. From the revolving door came a familiar voice:

"Well, hello, you two!"

Violet beamed at Robert. Muriel emerged from behind him. "And you brought your dog! How divine!"

"You know these people?" the straight-faced bellhop said.

"Of course." Robert shook Greg's hand. "They're very good friends."

"Don't they have a lovely dog?" Muriel said.

The smiling bellhop nodded.

The straight-faced bellhop scowled. "She's not allowed inside," he said.

"Then we won't take her inside," Greg said. "We'll visit with our friends out here."

"Away from the door," he grumbled. "You'll disturb the other guests."

"The lobby's empty," Robert said.

"Away from the door," the straight-faced bellhop repeated. "Now, before I get the clerk."

"All right, all right," Greg said. "We're going. No need to get cross…"

They left the door for the middle of the courtyard and stood about in the grass. Robert offered Muriel a cigarette. She took it between her lips and leaned into his lighter.

"What a stuffy place," Violet said. "Is it any better inside?"

Robert chuckled. "Not by much," he said. "The clerk at the front desk is a bit of an ass."

"No kidding," Greg said. "He laughed in my face when I tried to get us a room. They don't like dogs here, do they?"

"No, and it's a damned shame." Robert patted Izzy's head. Muriel handed him her cigarette and he took a puff from it himself. "They're misunderstood, especially in places like this."

"They are," Muriel said, kneeling down in the grass. She stroked Izzy's ears and planted a kiss on her snout. "You're a sweet girl, aren't you?" Izzy sniffed her words and kissed her face.

Greg laughed. "Don't spoil her too much," he joked. "Otherwise, she'll want to go home with you."

"That's fine," Muriel said. "She's lovely. We'll have lots of fun."

"She's beautiful," Robert said. "Maybe we should get a dog. We were never much for kids."

"We have nieces and nephews," Muriel reminded him. "They're more than enough."

"They're a handful," he agreed. "But she's not."

"She was when she was a puppy," Violet said. "My brother used to say that all the time."

Greg scratched Izzy's back. "She's still a puppy now—just on the inside."

"She has young eyes," Muriel said. "Look at them, Robert! They're young and bright."

"They're like yours," Robert said. "Except, hers are prettier."

Everyone laughed.

Muriel straightened up, nudging him playfully. "Give me back that cigarette. It's making you hazy..." He relinquished it and she took a puff. "Now," she said, smiling at Greg and Violet. "We have something for you."

"Oh, yes." Robert dug around in his pocket. "Just a little gift—a souvenir of our time here together." He withdrew his hand and opened it for them to see.

Violet smiled at the two corks in his palm. One was flared like a bell, and the other was a perfect cylinder.

"From Al Mare's," Greg said. "I'll be damned..."

Violet pointed at them. "Look at the lettering."

Robert turned them over in his hand. *PORTSMOUTH 1950* was scrawled across their sides.

"I'll be damned," Greg said again. "Thanks, you two."

"From the cava and the Côtes du Rhône," Robert said. "Two nights spent with two new friends."

Muriel grinned. "We couldn't have asked to spend them a better way."

Greg accepted the corks and shook Robert's hand. "It's been a pleasure getting to know you both," he said. "Thank you."

"For everything," Violet said. "You're wonderful people."

"Of course," Robert said. "Let's plan to come back here again. The next time we eat at Al Mare's, the bill is ours."

"Deal," Greg said.

They hugged all around. Izzy sat happily in the middle of them.

"Take care, you two," Robert said. "You want a ride back to your hotel?"

Greg swatted the air. "No, that's all right. We walked here to begin with—I'm sure we can walk back."

"You sure?" He glanced down at Izzy. "She looks tired."

Violet followed his gaze. Izzy looked up, panting. "She does, doesn't she? What do you think, Greg?"

He hesitated. "You sure it's not going to be any trouble?"

"Of course not," Muriel assured them. "It makes no sense to walk. Wait here, and he'll bring the car around."

Robert nodded and hurried off toward the hotel. A short while later, he pulled up to the curb in a gleaming black Cadillac. He rolled down the window. "Did someone call a taxi?"

Muriel opened the back door and let Izzy in first. Violet got in behind her, and Greg got in on the other side. Muriel sat up front with Robert. The inside of the car was beige and clean. It smelled faintly of tobacco.

"So..." Robert looked back at them. "Where's this hotel of yours?"

"Court Street," Greg said. "The Mariner's House, over in Strawberry Banke."

"The old neighborhood," Robert mused. He put the car in gear and pulled away from the curb. "There's great skating there in the winter. You ever been?"

"Once or twice," Violet said. "But that was years ago, before the war."

Muriel winked at them over her shoulder. "There's plenty of skating up in Canada," she said. "But Robert can't skate for his life..."

"That's enough out of you," Robert said. "And put out that cigarette, will you? I'm trying to drive..."

# 14

"Nice place," Robert said, when they got to The Mariner's House. "They take dogs, too?"

Violet smiled at Izzy. "This time, they did."

"The clerk's damned nice," Greg added. "Damned nice and damned reasonable. Nothing like the ass up the street."

"Excellent," Robert said. "The world could use more people like that."

Beside him, Muriel rummaged around in her purse. She withdrew a pen, and Greg took out the scrap of paper with the address of their hotel on it. "Perfect," she said, and scribbled something on the back. "We'll be back in Ottawa on Sunday. Call us anytime."

"We will," Violet said, as Greg tucked the paper away. "Come visit us in Maine. We live up along the coast, where it's quiet and beautiful. It'll be a wonderful time."

"We just might do that," Robert said. "The same goes for you. You're always welcome."

"And don't worry," Muriel said. "We take dogs."

Greg got out of the car first, followed by Violet and Izzy. "Take care."

"So long, you two." Muriel rolled up the window with a wink.

As they drove off, Robert honked the horn. Greg and Violet waved from the sidewalk as Izzy wagged her tail. The Cadillac disappeared around the corner of Pleasant and Court Street.

"I'll miss them," Violet said.

Greg smiled at the street corner. "I will, too."

They walked up the brick pathway to The Mariner's House and helped Izzy up the stairs to their room. She lay at the foot of the bed and watched them pack. Violet tossed her dirty dresses in with her clean ones, knowing that she'd wash them all once they were back home. She counted her sunhats to make sure she had them all and stacked them inside one another so they would fit inside her suitcase. She stuffed Izzy's bowl and what was left of her food into the remaining gaps of space, then closed her suitcase and clasped it shut.

Greg scanned the room for anything they could have forgotten. "Is that it?"

"I think so. You have the corks?"

"I have the corks."

"And their phone number?"

"And their phone number."

"Do you have the room key?"

"It's in my pocket."

"All right," she said. "I think that's everything."

Greg pursed his lips. "Wait—there's something we forgot."

"What's that?"

He was standing next to her and swooped in to kiss her cheek. She wrinkled her nose. "You're ridiculous…"

"All right," he said. "That's everything." He took his suitcase in one hand and Violet's in the other.

She took hold of Izzy's leash and coaxed her to her feet. "Ready, sweet girl?"

They drew the curtains and locked the door on their way out. Greg went downstairs first to take their luggage to the car.

"I'll meet you at the front desk."

"Sounds good to me."

She helped Izzy down the stairs, one step at a time. Izzy stumbled twice, but Violet was there to steady her. "I got you," she whispered, patting her side. When they reached the bottom, Izzy raised her head in triumph. Light shone on in her tired eyes.

Greg was just getting back from the car when they reached the front desk. The old clerk nodded at them.

"Here to check out?"

"Yes, sir."

"And did you enjoy your stay?"

Greg handed him the room key. "We did," he said. "All three of us."

The old clerk accepted the key and deposited it into a drawer behind his desk. He made a mark in his book and peered over at Izzy. "Wonderful," he said. "And I have to hand it to you—she behaved beautifully."

Violet grinned. "Didn't we tell you she would?"

"You did," he said. "But you never quite know with that type of thing."

"Thanks for giving us a chance," Greg said. "We'll never forget it."

"Neither will I." He reached over the desk and shook their hands. "The next time you're in Portsmouth, I'd be happy if you stayed here. I can't promise you the same room, but I can promise you a place to stay." He smiled. "Bye, now. It's been a pleasure."

They paid for the room and thanked him again. The old clerk wished them a safe trip home. They went out into the sunlight and down the brick pathway. Greg had the car running out by the hedges. Violet let Izzy in the back, smiling as she rested her head between the driver and passenger seats. She got in next, then Greg.

"Well," he said. "That's that."

"That's that," she said. "You think we'll ever come back?"

He considered The Mariner's House. "I think so. All in all, it was a great trip."

"It was," she said. "Bitter at parts, but better than I expected."

He nodded. "Like the first sip of Campari after a very long time away."

"Exactly. It's bitter at first, but then the bitterness begins to fade…" She settled back in her seat as he pulled away from the hedges. "And soon, it's nothing more than an aftertaste."

They drove to the corner of Court and Pleasant Street, and Greg met her gaze.

"You're thinking," she said.

He glanced in the rearview mirror. "I am."

Violet looked back. There was a car behind them. Greg turned right onto Pleasant Street. The other car went left.

"What do you say we spend a bit longer in Portsmouth?" he said. "We have all day to get home. Why don't we leave after lunch?"

She grinned. "Fine by me." They stopped at the intersection of Pleasant and State Street, alongside the busy cafés. "Where do you want to go?"

"Anywhere."

"What about Prescott Park?"

Greg turned onto State Street. "Sure."

They passed the Kingsbury House, its handsome brick walls adorned with ivy, and soon came upon Al Mare's. The host was outside on the terrace, opening up the umbrellas and arranging the chairs around the tables. A couple of waiters were helping him.

At the end of State Street, they turned onto Marcy Street and pulled into the dirt lot that faced the Liberty Pole. Greg and Violet got out first, then helped Izzy out after. She yawned and wagged her tail. Violet patted her side.

They crossed the road and followed the sidewalk beside the wrought iron fence. Beyond the fence, Prescott Park was as beautiful as ever. The grass and the flowerbeds were done up with dew, and the cascading water of the fountain was glittering in the sun. The breeze was cool and steady from the harbor, and there was a softness to the sighing of the trees. The seasons were shifting and their leaves would soon be lost, but they didn't seem to be the least bit shaken by it. Violet admired their tranquility. Acceptance was the emblem of the fall.

They sat on a bench by the roses, and Izzy laid down in the grass. She looked about and sniffed the air and was happy. Greg and Violet watched her for a while. People waved at her as they went past.

"You know," Greg said, smiling at Izzy. "She's kind of like our rose, isn't she?"

Violet nodded, surveying the white parts of her black fur. "It's times like these when I wish roses bloomed forever..."

"That's not what I was getting at," he said.

"I know—but I still wish they did."

He paused. "Our rose hasn't lost its petals yet."

"No." She stroked Izzy's back. "Not yet."

"Hey," he said, and she met his eyes. "Roses don't last forever. We know that." He placed his hand over hers. "But ours is here right now. That's worth its weight in gold."

Violet managed a smile. Greg's words were as warm as his touch, and Izzy's breathing was slow and serene. She gave both of them a kiss. Greg offered her his hand.

"Al Mare's?" he said.

She stood up from the bench. "Al Mare's."

They strolled back to the wrought iron fence, leaving the park behind. Izzy wagged her tail as she walked. There was autumn in her eyes.

At Al Mare's, there were plenty of empty tables and they sat on the terrace facing the street. A waiter brought them menus and set a bowl of water down for Izzy. She drank sloppily and laid down at their feet. Greg and Violet laughed. The waiter was less amused.

"What did he expect?" Greg said, dabbing Izzy's mouth with his napkin. "She's a dog—how else is she supposed to drink?"

Violet lifted the bowl away, placing it on one of the empty chairs. "Your guess is as good as mine…"

The waiter returned with a jug of water for the table and a couple more napkins. He took out his notepad and asked what they would have. Greg ordered a bowl of tomato bisque and a loaf of focaccia to share. Violet had the caprese salad. It was tossed with bits of fresh mozzarella and drizzled with balsamic vinaigrette. Afterward, they had coffee.

Violet smiled into her cup. She had forgotten how good the coffee was at Al Mare's. It was a full-bodied Americano—bold and robust, as smooth as it was bitter.

"Some of the best coffee in Portsmouth," Greg said, setting his cup on the table. There was still half a loaf of focaccia left, and he divided it down the middle with his knife. They took their time eating the rest of it, dipping their slices into the bowl of seasoned olive oil. It paired wonderfully with the coffee. They ordered another cup.

Violet leaned back in her chair as the bells of the Old North Church rang out the time. She didn't catch all of the tolls, and what she did hear was muffled by the low hum of the traffic. The steeple, after all, was several blocks away. She looked at Greg.

He checked his watch. "Noon."

She sipped her coffee. "Lovely."

They sat in silence, drinking in the peace of the terrace and watching the cars go down the street. In the distance was the Memorial Bridge. On the opposite side of the bridge was Maine.

Greg cleared his throat. "What do you say, Vi? After this, should we go home?"

She considered the bridge over the rim of her cup. "That depends," she said.

"On what?"

"On which home you're talking about."

He gave her a funny look. "What do you mean?"

"You know what I mean, Greg."

"I don't think I do," he said. "We only have one."

"We had Bill's," she said.

"That was before the war..."

She nodded.

"We sold it," he reminded her.

"We could still go back."

He looked at her and drank some coffee. "You want to?"

She shrugged.

"I didn't think you wanted to."

"In the beginning, I didn't," she admitted. "But now, after everything, I feel like we might as well."

He rubbed his forehead with the palm of his hand. "All right, but—what changed?"

"I don't know," she said. She thought of Hampton—of the loneliness and bitterness and torn-up feelings, and of all the things that had made it that way. "I guess I feel like if we don't go now, we probably never will."

"You're probably right," he said.

"I don't know," she said again. "Maybe I'm wrong. Maybe a year from now, we'll take a visit with Robert and Muriel."

"No," Greg said. "We won't do that. That sounds like hell."

"It wouldn't be so bad. They'd be there. They'd liven it up."

"I don't know, Vi. It still sounds like hell."

The waiter came by to drop off their check and cleared away some of their dishes. They paid the check and put down a tip. Violet drank the rest of her coffee. Greg finished his as Izzy napped beneath the table.

He sighed. "All right..."

"What?"

"I know you're right. If we don't go back today, we might not go back at all."

Violet shrugged. "All I'm saying is we might as well."

"Yeah, I know. We should. For us, and for her."

He nudged Izzy's tail with his foot. She yawned, stood, and shook herself awake. Violet took hold of her leash.

The three of them left the terrace and set off down State Street. The sign above Al Mare's watched them go.

# 15

When they got back to the car, they let Izzy in the back before getting in themselves. Greg started the engine and met Violet's gaze. "You're sure you want to do this?"

She took a deep breath, answering with her eyes. Izzy was falling asleep beside her.

"We don't have to," he said.

"I know, but we might as well. It's been long enough."

He held out his hand and she squeezed it. He squeezed hers back.

They backed out of the dirt lot onto Marcy Street and drove alongside Prescott Park. The trees were sturdy sentinels of change.

Greg took a right down Hancock Street, followed it through Strawberry Banke, and turned onto Pleasant Street by the statue of Fitz John Porter. They passed the John Langdon House shortly afterward, then turned left onto Junkins Ave.

The South Mill Pond, framed by rosehips and beach roses, marked their ascent of the hill near City Hall. At the top of the hill, they drove on toward Rye. The white steeple of the

Old North Church was now behind them. They were headed back home.

They took the same back way as the day before, pausing at the four-way intersection that led into Hampton. Violet glanced left, toward the sea. Greg waited for a car to pass, then continued straight through. The road into Hampton was wooded and winding. Clearings opened up in the trees, revealing old colonial homesteads and their low-lying stone walls. They passed the Simon Lane House on their right and, not long after, the rust-colored barn of the Wayside Farm.

Violet closed her eyes, anticipating the house that would soon come up on their right. It would be quite a distance from the road, waiting for them at the end of a long dirt driveway. The last time they had seen it was when they had left it, in the fall of '45. Before then, they had built a life there with Bill and Izzy. Then the war had happened and things had changed. Bill had died, Izzy had grown old, and it hurt just as much to be in Hampton—but that house had always been their home.

She supposed that was the way it went. The world changed, and life went on. People lived and loved and died. Grief was an endless road. The horizon was hard to make out, but it was still there. Home was home, even when it stopped feeling like it.

She kept her eyes closed as they approached and felt them slow down. They turned and Greg brought them to a stop. He idled for a moment, heaved a sigh, and cut the engine. In the ensuing silence, he placed his hand over hers. She opened her eyes at the hesitance of his touch. Immediately, she wished she hadn't.

Bill's driveway was now a long stretch of pavement that ended in a cul-de-sac. His house was gone. An entirely new neighborhood stood in its place.

Violet shook her head at everything. Every inch of her was numb. She got out of the car. Greg did, too.

They stood and stared and didn't say much of anything. Then Violet remembered Izzy and got her out of the back. She looked around and looked up at them. Violet winced at the light in her eyes, knowing full well that none of it was reflected in theirs. She held Izzy's leash in one hand and Greg's hand in the other. Her grasp on both was limp. Her heart was heavy. She willed herself to move forward, but it all felt so pointless.

Greg took the first steps. She and Izzy followed.

They wandered to the cul-de-sac at the end of the street, unnerved by the new houses. They were almost identical to the ones surrounding the land that had once been their air-field—white, neat, and modular. The only difference was that these had garages, and their yards were more generously appor-tioned. Everything else about them was the same—the rooftop TV antennas, the gated picket fences, and the monochromatic mailboxes out front. They were all, at the moment, unoccupied. Their owners were almost certainly at work.

Violet lingered in the middle of the cul-de-sac, vaguely aware of their closeness to where Bill's house had been. She stared at the ground beneath her feet, searching herself for any memory that could offer her some sense of solace. She couldn't think of any good ones, and the bad ones all felt meaningless. Home had never seemed so far away.

They walked back to the car and helped Izzy into the back. Violet shut the door and bowed her head. Greg opened his arms and she leaned into them. He stroked her hair and rubbed her back, and she figured he was waiting in case she started to cry. She didn't. She was too numb to cry. She had no tears—and no words, either.

She held onto him until she got tired of standing in the street. When she stepped back, she raised her face to the sky. Behind the clouds, the sun was the color of Campari. The neighborhood was lonely below.

Greg grimaced. "Did you see what they called it?"

"No."

He gestured at the telephone pole closest to the car. Protruding from the side, about halfway up, was a small green sign with white lettering.

*MASLOW TERRACE,* it said.

She felt a stab of grief, then altogether empty.

"Bastards," Greg said.

They turned away and got back into the car. Izzy had already drifted off to sleep. She lifted her head when Greg started the engine. Violet rested her hand by her snout, comforted by her slow and peaceful sighs. They left the neighborhood behind and headed down the road.

Greg glanced at her from the steering wheel. "Should we talk about it?"

"I don't know, Greg. I don't think there's much to say."

"No," he said. "I guess there isn't."

They passed the old barn of the Wayside Farm, under the shadows of the trees.

A little while after, Violet sighed. "It's really over now, isn't it?"

"Yes," he said. "It really is."

They drove on and fell silent, resigning themselves to the end of it. Izzy slept on between them. The road was long and shaded.

**Michael Lajoie** is a faithful coffee drinker, jazz listener, and local history lover. His other works include *The Summit by the Sea* (2020) and *As Way Leads onto Way* (2022). He lives in Seacoast New Hampshire with his family.

9 798218 050528

Jim Parkes

Typeset in Trebuchet using OpenOffice.org

**All author royalties from the sale of
this book will be donated to ChildLine.**

*The pace of life today can be relentless. This amusing fictitious novel gives an insight into how your life could be more peaceful. Check out what the main character finds between the CD and DVD shelves at the supermarket that changes his whole approach to life, love and everything in between.*

*This is dedicated to my wonderful four children Stephen, Katherine, Rachel and Elizabeth. You continue to be a source of pleasure and joy to me; I love you deeply and treasure each one of you. Kindred spirits reaching out to each other across the decades, outside of time itself, I will always hold you in my arms as I will also hold your children and your children's children.*

*Love, Dad x*

# PRAISE

*"This book will show you how to get the most out of yourself, and others, for the rest, and the best, of your life."*
**Brian Tracy, Author, The Way To Wealth,**
**www.briantracyinternational.com**

*"This book is 'unputdownable'! I just couldn't stop reading. I read it on my birthday - sitting on the grass enjoying the glorious summer sunshine and looking out to sea, over sand dunes and green fields. What a gift - days later it's still popping into my mind. A great book packed full of great analogies, common sense, practical tips and fun - Jim's warmth and humour shine through every page. It's too good to keep to yourself - you'll want to pass it on. This is essential reading for all peace-takers everywhere - are you ready to take the peace?"*
**Mary Collin, Life MInstD, Founder President, Professional Speakers Association (Midlands), www.marycollin.co.uk**

*"Hi Jim, An interesting read, I took the decision to alter my life totally in 1998 and having come through some taut times, am now more relaxed, unstressed and 'at peace' than ever before. Cheers and all good things."*
**Bob Carolgees, British TV and cabaret entertainer for 25 years**

*"I love this book. It is easy to read, containing powerful messages. I would highly recommend this book to anyone interested in personal development."*
**Tony Burgess, Director, The Academy of High Achievers, www.aha-success.com**

*"A lovely story you do not want to put down, or finish, as it really makes you think. Cheers!"*
**Barry Phillips, owner and manager, www.knowledgeisking.co.uk**

*"The great teachers of this planet have told us that life is an illusion that we create. Quantum physics teaches us that if we observe something, we change it. We are all so busy dealing with the distractions of our illusion that we forget that we are human beings and not human doings. This book will remind you of your true nature and how to take the journey that leads you back to that which is within you. Follow the techniques in the book and find the peace that each one of us and humanity desperately needs. It is time for a change. It begins with YOU. Remember, you could be 'The Hundredth Monkey'!!!"*
**Ron Violet, Doctor of Naturopathy, Energy Worker and Student on the Planet for Slow Learners**

*"It is a really thought provoking story and easy to read. It also shows you how you can move on in your life. Fantastic!"*
**Paul and Sarah Barton, Business owners Sugars4life, www.sugars4life.com**

*"An engaging story, and an inspiring reminder that positive personal action can create real and peaceful changes in our world."*
**Brian Carr, Chief Executive, BVSC: The Centre for Voluntary Action**

*"Written in the true spirit of a 'Beginners Mind', this book talks you through making first steps into the vast world of personal development. Food for body, mind and spirit."*
**Thera Tolner, Sky Coaching & Consulting Limited**

*"I finished the book! Its such a lovely look at life, perspective and priority. We all need more peace and Inner peace is the most challenging to achieve! Thank you for creating a glimpse of it for everyone! Shopping will never be the same! God bless all you do, your heart and your spirit are a joy! Lots of love."*
**Kimberley Gridley, Business Developer and Entrepreneur**

# ACKNOWLEDGEMENTS

## A SHOPPING LIST OF THANKYOU'S

"Seriously, Are You Taking The Peace?" has been a special personal project for me. It would not be in existence now without a tremendous amount of love, hard work, skill and talent from a whole bunch of people in a focused short timeframe. Their spirit, passion and expertise have taken a vision and created the book you now have. These people are diamonds that I have the joy of knowing and sharing time with. I want to take this opportunity to give them the recognition they deserve. Hugs, Jim x

Special thanks to

- Elaine Collier for her encouragement and support in March 2006 to take the conceptual idea and convert that into a book. The draft manuscript was completed before the end of March 2006.

- My publishers, Debs Jenkins and Joe Gregory of Bookshaker.com, for their immediate energy and acceptance of the draft manuscript plus their willingness to change plans in order to achieve a September 2006 release.

- Kate Copestake for helping me to move this to Final Draft by mid June 2006

- Sally Holliday for being a fantastic photographer! On a baking hot day in late June 2006, Sally made my first ever photo session such a laugh!

- Debs and Joe for their continued love, support and energy throughout this whole project, balancing other work commitments and still finding the time to work on the script, the illustrations, artwork and book cover design, the Peacetakers.com website and more.

- Eric Kent and Sanita Guddu from ChildLine, Midlands and East Anglia, for their wonderful care and support on this remarkable journey.

- A very special thank you to Lesley Parkes, Rachel and Elizabeth for your patience and understanding as I have spent many hours in the office with this project.

- Debs Jenkins, not only a fantastic publisher, but also a dear friend, a buddy. A true shining light that comes from within and spreads light to everyone.

- Finally, to my family and friends. Without your love and support this would not have been possible. Thank you all from the bottom of my heart.

Praise

Acknowledgements

Contents

----------------------------------------

----------------------------------------

# PROLOGUE

September is always a special time for me; it brings thoughts of "New Beginnings". A time when the lazy days of summer gracefully take a bow and move gently aside to let autumn take centre stage. A time for change, a reminder that life doesn't stand still. Children returning to school in new uniforms. Relieved parents, as the home becomes a place of peace again after the summer's excitement and activities. Or, a time to do the packing for a holiday now that the school term has started. Holiday resorts are more peaceful and life can be lived at a more leisurely pace. Whatever setting we are in the one thing we all want is some peace.

Many people campaign for World peace, a desire for peace in our times. How many of us are proactive about peace at an individual level. How much peace is in our lives – right now?

Before we can answer that question there is a need to give definition to this word, because, that's all it is, a word until we give it shape and function. The dictionary starts to give us a glimpse into this – period free from war, calmness, quietness, lack of anxiety. I wonder if these are the words that we would use to describe our lives at the moment.

*A Period Free from War – personal war*

Yes, we can look at this from a macro perspective, but what about from a personal level? Let's consider this from *our* world, not *the* world. Being in that heightened adrenalin state, having to constantly battle between the choice of fight or flight hour by hour, every day of our lives.

What would a period free from war mean to us right now?

What possibilities or opportunities would that bring our way, and how would life be different if that were possible? To stop being our own war correspondent, always reporting how it is from the front line.

What would it mean to us to be at peace right now?

*A Period Free from War – with a partner*

Our war may be mental, physical, sexual or emotional, or in some cases all of them. It's hard to accept, but every day we make choices to stay in that dark place. What if things could be different? There are many organisations set up to help someone in these situations. It is easy to think that we are the only person going through this pain. This could not be further from the truth, there are many people out there suffering. But there is hope. There are Professionals who are waiting to help you, all you need to do is ask.

What would it mean to you to be at peace right now?

*A Period Free from War – with close family & friends*

We all need people around us who are on our side, our support system when things go wrong. These are the people you know you can count on. So what happens when we are in a war zone with these special people? It's like being on a high wire and someone removes the safety net. We feel alone and very vulnerable.

What would it mean to you to be at peace with these people right now?

*A Period Free from War - within your work environment*

How different would work be without all the internal battles between staff? How much more efficient would we be without having to tread daily through a minefield? Would we like to work in a reduced stress environment where there was an excellent team spirit? A place where efforts were genuinely recognised and rewarded? What if such a place could exist, what if this could be reality, our reality?

What would it mean to us to be at peace with these people right now?

*Calmness*

A picture of a calm sea, just the gentleness of the natural rhythm of the waves of the ocean as it wraps around a boat like a mother lovingly rocking a baby. We use the expression "the calm before the storm" knowing that the power of the ocean is ever present. We are reminded of the constant danger that the sea holds, how many people have lost their lives and the lives of their loved ones over the centuries. What would it mean to you to be able to sail through life and not feel like you are just flotsam and jetsam being tossed about in a storm?

We all know the expression, "we are all in the same boat", actually we are not. We are all in our *own* boats and what makes the difference is the person who is steering.

I'm not saying that life can be all plain sailing, but the question needs to be asked whether you are enjoying or enduring your life's cruise. If it's the latter, maybe you need to brush up on your sailing techniques.

## Quietness

Quietness – the opposite of noise. Our lives are full of noise, to the point that some people must have background noise all their waking hours. What noises are going on inside you? That voice you hear that says, "You're not good enough, you're not smart enough, you couldn't possibly do that …" You know that voice; you've heard it many times. It attacks your self-confidence and leaves doubts wherever it goes.

If you are reading this and thinking, "what a load of rubbish, I don't think that", that's the voice I'm talking about. How about if you heard "Mirror, Mirror on the wall, who is the fairest of them all?" Is your immediate reaction – ME! – or do you think of someone else? There's that voice again!

## Lack of Anxiety

A lack of fear and worry; these are two major players in the health of our nation in this millennium. What would life be like without being chained to these stresses?

Having peace is not a passive activity it's a choice, a choice that we make every day. We choose each morning what clothes we will wear. Granted some people's wardrobe range may be more extensive than ours, but I don't see many naked people walking around the streets of this country.

Also, consider the many culinary choices available to us daily. From traditional to the exotic. Food that will complement our mood, or the people and circumstances we find ourselves with at that moment. Life is about choices. Finding the available options and making a choice.

What follows is a light-hearted look at one man's journey to find peace – peace in a box.

Jim Parkes

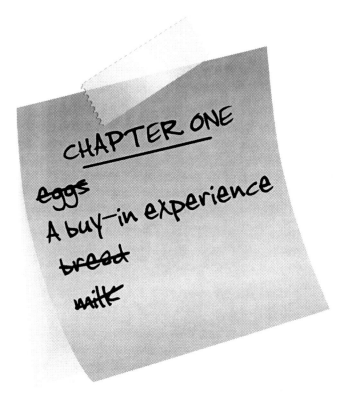

Like most people, during the month of January, I'm taking some time to consider the past year and what the coming one may bring my way. I've lived my whole life rushing around from one situation to the next.

I did that until one day last year when I saw someone actually pick up *peace* off the shopping shelves of life. It was there all the time; I just couldn't see it.

As always, I'm so excited I've started this story in the middle, so let me share this story with you from the beginning.

This all started just five months ago in September of last year. Previous to that, like most people, I had a busy lifestyle and liked to fit as much in as I could. I'm one of those people that said phrases like "I work hard, so I can play hard" or "Sleep? Why would I want to sleep? That's the closest I get to being dead". You know the type.

To me, there is nothing pleasurable about shopping for food or household items; it's one of the necessary evils that we all have to do.

I've tried altering the day and the time I do it – I just hate it.

A new retail chain store had opened up one of those 24-hour shops so I've even tried the nightmare activity at 3am in the morning – the place is filled with the living dead!

I write lists before I go. You've guessed that. I stick to the list and it limits the torture. I've always got a pound coin for the trolley. I still haven't forgiven the tight git who ripped me off with a forgery.

I take a few good deep breaths in front of the automatic doors. I move my hands inside the trolley handles, battle scars from previous experiences remind me that it's not clever to have your hands on the outside. I mentally put on my American football style crash helmet and then the voice in my head says, "It's time... go, go, go" and then I join the masses.

Now, on this night in September, I could see the few shoppers like me who knew exactly what they wanted. I could see the masses of casual shoppers and the "let's take the family out for the whole day" shoppers. When I was less than five metres through the doors the back nearside wheel started to wobble, and make an annoying grating sound. People were looking at me as if it was my fault. I kicked it, nothing happened. Should I abandon this defective equipment, abort the mission or carry on?

I carried on … Up and down the aisles I filled the trolley with the provisions I needed. Cereal, 3rd aisle on the right. Toilet rolls, 5th aisle on the left. Oh no, it was September, that meant all the Christmas stock was on the shelves and everything had changed around. I was now in major panic mode, I had no idea where anything was. I had to resort to looking at the overhead signs.

If that's not enough, there were signs on the floor too. My body was reacting like a diver who is running out of oxygen and doesn't think there will be sufficient to get to the surface. My list was ticked off; I was ticked off and ready to get out of the place. I headed towards the checkout, every one of them had a massive queue ... ARRRHHHH!

At this point I took a few deep calming breaths knowing that I'd soon be out, mission accomplished. I joined one of the queues. Then it happened as it always does, the checkout queues either side of mine moved so fast leaving me literally standing there watching others leave the store as the intercom was heard relaying the message "Supervisor to checkout 13, thank you."

Finally it was my turn, but no, I had to wait again as there's ice cream all over the conveyor belt. Two minutes and two metres of tissue paper later I was asked, "Do you want help with your packing?"

"No" – I threw the items back into the trolley, I "chipped & pinned" and headed straight out of the exit. On the way out I heard "Are you interested in a conservatory?" The salesman got a short, sharp answer delivered as I raced for the door.

After a final kick of the trolley wheel, it was parked and as I put the £1 coin in my pocket I punched the air and shouted – "YES, mission accomplished"!

--X--

Every time we grocery shop we walk down the aisles and make conscious choices. These days on-line shopping choices are made and cyber-space trolleys filled, and at least you don't get the one with the dodgy wheels.

There are no surprises when we get to the checkout, whatever items we have chosen are what we get. If you don't consciously take something off the shelf, it's not going to be in your basket or trolley.

Shopping is one of the world's greatest levellers. We all do it in one way or the other and you know that you will see a cross-section of the population in the supermarket at any one time. Some use my smash and grab method, whilst others use the venue as a place to meet new people in a non–threatening environment with the added advantage of seeing their shopping preferences (would you choose your potential life partner depending on the type of toothpaste they buy?) Stranger things do happen, as you will soon get to find out.

Once at home the job is still not complete. It's now time for the restocking to commence. Items placed in the cupboards in "use by" chronological date order, labels facing exactly forward, jars and tins in size order. Fridge and freezer food rotated efficiently and the contents list updated so I always know what I have to use. Is this really me? No way, life is too short for all that. I have the lucky dip approach to food in cupboards. Many times my culinary choice has been whatever falls out of the cupboard!

Now the food is away, the kitchen cupboards are groaning under the weight, it's a miracle that they are still attached to the walls. I've fought my way out of the chest freezer. You know, there are things inside there that I have no idea what they are. I've had a longer relationship with some of that frozen food than I did with my ex–partner.

Ah, my ex–partner, a 34-year old vision of beauty. She had the looks, the personality, the high-powered job, the

BMW and all the latest fashions. Men loved her and other women just couldn't stand her. I was the proudest man in the world when we went out and she was on my arm. Friends would say to me, "Why is she with you?" I knew they were all jealous; this was the single, smart, sexy and successful woman who walked into my life just two years ago and stole my heart.

However, just a short time ago, with the aid of a legal associate, she stole my bank balance too.

Two years ago, she looked so good wearing my shirt when she stayed over one night, now it doesn't feel so good that she wanted everything, including the shirt off my back. Yes, I have been taken to the cleaners and been left picking up the bill. Was I bitter about this? Of course I was. I'd lost everything apart from the contents of the chest freezer.

I thought, "I must get around to throwing some of that stuff away." I'm sure it's breaking some EU regulation to have food that long.

As I sat trying to bring the feeling back into my now cold fingers, which resemble a pack of frozen sausages (with just the same amount of dexterity) I could feel my blood boil as I shouted at the empty space she left behind, "I hate you as much as I hate shopping!"

Little did I know that by mid October my shopping missions would never be the same again, ever – but even more important than that, neither would I.

Jim Parkes

It all happened late on a Thursday evening at the 24-hour supermarket. It was twenty one hundred hours as I entered the store with my list in one hand and a look of determination on my face. I was so focused on my mission that I didn't see the "slippery surface" sign in aisle 3. I thought it was strange to be able to smell the lavender and camomile as I walked past detergents, but naively I put this down to a store "promotion" pumping the smell through the air conditioning in an attempt to encourage customers to purchase the item.

That was until I slipped in such a comical way and of course to me it was all in slow motion.

My feet were the first to go, just like you see in cartoons as a kid. My hands holding onto the trolley for all the good that did, because the trolley was also travelling through the fabric conditioner. Within seconds the trolley was tipped up and the contents were flying everywhere.

I don't remember trying to catch the jar of pickled onions, but the CCTV captured this spectacular feat. It was that action that won me first prize when the footage was sent into the TV Programme "You've been... caught on film doing stupid things." In carrying out this incredible action I failed to see the large pyramid-shaped display of washing liquid pockets. The force with which I hit this sent a shower of these little green pockets up into the air. Hundreds of individual little green "hailstones" showered down on the shoppers in aisle 4 as security cameras rolled.

As I drifted in and out of a state of consciousness I noticed a large crowd of people gathering around me. The next thing I heard was a voice saying, "Please move out of the way, I'm a first aider." Like a hurting child on hearing their mother's voice I knew that I would be okay. What I hadn't considered was that my rescuer was in fact a fork-lift truck driver and he was still driving his machine at the time.

My vision was blurred but I saw the crowd part and the fork lift truck getting closer to me. I felt the cold metal of the forks go under my back and lift me up like a rag doll from the floor. For some reason known only to the driver it was safer for me to be lifted to a height above 2 metres and transported out of the aisles.

My recollection of this incident is very patchy, all I can remember is that I felt like I was in a scene from the movie "King Kong" as my limp body lay in the "arms" of this mighty beast.

King Kong laid me down gently on the conveyor belt at the express checkout. I looked up and I saw blinding light, I thought, "This is it, the final check-out for me." Then I realised that I was seeing a blinding green light. I was always told that you saw a white light as you moved from this world to the next. Then it struck me, I was staring up at the barcode scanning beam and there was an error message flashing on the LED display.

I was checked out and thankfully I was okay. King Kong made light of it by saying "you are in a stable condition(er)."

It was time to re-evaluate my mission in the light of the recent events.

Should I abort or push forward to completion? I decided to regroup my thoughts and consider the available options.

I chose my location carefully for this major planning activity and made my way to the supermarket restaurant.

As I sat drinking my third cup of black coffee my eyes glanced across at aisle 13 and noticed something very unusual. I rubbed my eyes and looked again, it was still there. I'd never seen this on the shelf before, is this for real or were my eyes deceiving me. I walked over and yes, there was a row of boxes nestled between the CDs and DVDs and the shelf was labelled "Peace In A Box". Around me shoppers were looking at the CDs and DVDs but no one seemed to have noticed the Peace boxes.

As I reached for one of the boxes I had a weird but very strong gut reaction – this is what was missing in my life. The first thing I noticed was a very glossy brilliant white box with no writing – the description was only on the shelf itself. To my surprise the box was light, which is a strange thing to say as I had no concept of the weight I should expect peace to be.

As I examined the box there was in fact writing on it; embossed white letters that said "PEACE IN A BOX –

individual portion" and on the base there was a barcode. This prompted me to look for a price; there was nothing on the box or the shelf either. How intriguing!

What was even more interesting was the fact that the people all around me were unaware that I was holding this box. Like a child with a wrapped present I shook it, there was no sound. I smelt it, there was no smell. It appeared to be an empty box. Is this some sort of a store promotion gimmick, was I being filmed again as a sick sort of joke, had I not suffered enough? As I looked around there were no cameras on me, no assistants looking at me; how bizarre, I thought.

I looked to see if others had noticed me picking up this special item on the shelf, and guess what? They hadn't. They literally just didn't get it! An elderly couple walked past me; they must have seen my accident because they asked me if I was "alright now". I said "yes", and then I showed them the peace in a box. They looked at me for a moment, then gave each other a knowing look and walked away saying to each other, "I think he should go to hospital, he's obviously still in shock."

I was totally confused by all of this and I felt the need for some fresh air. I had my box of peace and I headed towards the checkout. The assistant smiled as the display read "Free of Charge". Then I walked out. My brain was saying "what's all this about?" but I hadn't got the time to think about it; I couldn't wait to see what was inside the box. By the light from the orange neon above the bench I sat on, I noticed on the side of the box: "For lasting results Best Before: you get home."

I was now incensed with curiosity and intrigue. I ripped open the box and looked inside.

It was... empty.

I was so bitterly disappointed; I don't know about peace, the red mist of anger and rage had just descended. In disgust I threw the box in the bin next to me, and as I did I noticed other discarded peace boxes already in there, which just confirmed that this was indeed a hoax.

But, just as I was about to leave, I noticed a small piece of paper right in the very bottom corner of the box. I reached down and pulled out this piece of paper. It said in white embossed letters that were difficult to read "You already have what you seek within you."

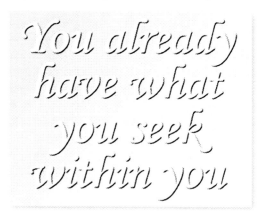

I thought "what a con!" - but then I had another thought, could the very thing that I'd been looking for the whole of my life really be inside of me, but buried so deep I didn't know it was there? I turned the paper over and it just said again in white embossed letters, "The treasure is within you", as if it knew that I needed further confirmation.

# The Treasure is within YOU

This whole experience left me feeling dazed and confused; I pushed the piece of paper in my pocket and drove home as quickly as I could. My home was not too far away and at that time of night the roads were quite quiet. As long as the traffic lights are on my side I can usually be home in minutes. I was soon in the comfort of my own home relaxing. It was now 11pm and the events of the last two hours were spinning around in my head. What if I was suffering from concussion? I decided that if I didn't feel better in the morning, I'd go to casualty just to make sure.

The alarm clock broke into my sleep. I turned it off and was thankful that I had booked this Friday off work to have a long weekend. As I pulled the quilt over my head the only sadness was that I had not remembered to turn off the alarm before going to bed, but with the events of last night it's hardly surprising that I had forgotten.

I turned over and fell asleep, going into a strange re-run in my mind of the accident in the supermarket and then seeing this Peace in a box and the cryptic message on the paper. I woke up with that phrase in my thoughts "You already have what you seek within you". Do you ever get that feeling when you're waking up, that you are never quite sure whether you are still in a dream or if this is now the real world? The rumbling in my stomach reminded me that this was the real world and I was hungry.

I stumbled downstairs in a sleepy state, opened the fridge door and grabbed the new six-pint milk container. In my book that's enough exercise for the triceps and biceps for anyone. Then I tried to open this miracle of modern science. You would have thought that this should be an easy operation, a plastic bottle with a plastic lid. But, oh no, some sadistic robot in a factory somewhere tightened every one of these stupid containers as tight as robotically possible and then gave it a further quarter twist just for luck. At this point the skin on my thumb and forefinger resembled the knurled thread on the outside of the lid and the top third of the container now looked like a Picasso sculpture of a naked woman's body!

It was time to get tough – where were the tea towels? One towel rolled and tied around my head in traditional Rambo style and the other wrapped around my still functioning hand. I sneaked up from behind the bottle and tried again.

Again I was defeated by the robot's strength. There was nothing to do but to continue the Rambo theme. I drew the largest knife out of the knife block, and, with a swift movement and a hint of October sunlight as it struck the blade, the decapitated milk lid and part of the container were now lying defeated on the floor. Another stunning victory of man over the robot.

Continuing in the same vein now as I was well and truly into the character, within seconds, the cornflakes box lid was lying next to the milk top, both having submitted to the skill and sheer brute force of Rambo. The tea towel was removed from my brow and cast over the items on the floor and as I walked back upstairs it dutifully absorbed the spilt milk.

As I sat in bed, munching through the bowl of cereal, my thoughts drifted away. All through my life I'd hankered after many things that I thought would enhance me; that would satisfy me. Without exception, these material things have all given me satisfaction to a degree, but nothing was sustainable.

Even the relationships I've had have never provided me with that peace of mind. I've always thought that there was someone out there that was my perfect match, that I'm not complete without them, there's a void in my life that will only be filled by that special person. Only then will I be at peace. But what if I don't meet them? Am I destined to live an unfulfilled life? Is it possible that what I seek is actually within me already? Do I have the capability to be whole without trying to find someone else to fill the gap? Do I get another bowl of cornflakes?

This last question appeared to be the simplest one for my sore brain to handle at that moment. The tea towel downstairs had completed its mission of absorbing all the spilt milk. I rescued it with my barbeque tongs and placed it in the sink to be dealt with later.

I say barbeque tongs, when what I really mean is a family heirloom passed onto me from my grandmother. This dear woman, who had lost the plot during her later years, left them to me in her will. These wooden tongs, the "high-tech" of her day, were used to move the laundry from wash side to the spin side of the labour saving device called a twin tub. I remembered grandma used to pretend to bite the backs of my ankles with it, chasing me round the house with her "crocodile". I could sense her doing this now as I returned upstairs with another full bowl of cereal.

Again, thoughts filled my head as I ate. I'd lived my whole life looking for external experiences to give me peace but to no avail. One of the things I remembered as I travelled home last night was a billboard advertising a personal development celebrity with a phrase that struck a chord with me: "If you always do what you've always done, you'll always get what you always got!"

Such a simple phrase that I've heard a thousand times but never gave it the thought that it actually deserved. I thought about it again; does it strike a chord with you?

There's another famous quote from Albert Einstein; "Insanity: doing the same thing over and over again and expecting different results."

If I continue to live my life the way I had been doing, it would be crazy to expect that I would get different results. To get different results, it makes sense that I needed to do different things.

Maybe this time I should stop doing things for an easy life and instead just be ME. But who am I really? You know I had never really spent any time thinking about who I was and what I wanted. It sounds stupid I know, but I had goals and targets set at work that I needed to reach in order to develop and get that pay rise, but I didn't actually do the same in my personal life.

I know the principles of setting personal goals, writing them down and monitoring progress. I normally did that at the start of each year but by February, LIFE always seemed to take over and that exercise went out of the window with all the other good intentions and New Year resolutions.

I compensated by always having to be out there working or playing hard. Life was meant for living and living in the fast lane, pedal to the metal and all those old clichés.

As I looked around my bedroom my eyes were drawn to the bookcase and to one book in particular, the First Aid Manual. I quickly flicked through to the section on concussion just to make sure that I was okay. Yeah, I was okay. But where were all these questions in my head coming from? As I flicked through the First Aid Manual I noticed the section about "The aims of First Aid", it says:

- To preserve life
- To limit worsening of the condition
- To promote recovery

I thought about King Kong; he'd certainly achieved those aims last night with me. There was something else going on now that may promote recovery in more than a physical sense.

--X--

Normally I can't stand silence. I need to have background noise from the time I wake to the time I go to bed so it's strange that I actually sat quietly and thought deeply about me. The more I thought, the more I realised that somewhere in the midst of living life I'd lost sight of me; the real me. The me, who as a kid wanted to do so many things, had so many hopes and dreams.

I wanted to be Captain James T Kirk on missions across the galaxy. Exploring new worlds, meeting new creatures and saying, "We come in Peace".

With state of the art technology communicator (made from a cook's matchbox) and phaser (made from a plastic lemon juice container) I must have looked like a demented male cat "spraying" everything in the back garden. However to me, these were strange new worlds I was exploring.

Here we are a few decades later with people walking around with personal communicators (mobile phones) and even more surprisingly, you can see people with Lieutenant Uhura ear appendages (Bluetooth).

For the love of Star Trek, beam me up Scotty, "There's life Jim, but not as we know it!"

How do we stay alive in this 21st century? O yes, Staying Alive... reminds me of my late teens, I was John Travolta in Saturday Night Fever.

You should have seen me on the dance floor at the local disco, Tiffany's. White suit, big collars and platform boots. Unfortunately, I didn't own a pair of platforms at that time so I "borrowed" my older brother's without him knowing. Now my feet stopped growing at the age of 14, a petite size 6, he was a size 8. With socks pushed down to fill the gaps and a little practice I could walk in them. With even more practice, I could dance in them.

Well that was until one occasion when I was in dancing competition with a large circle of people watching me. One of the oversized platform boots decided to leave my dainty foot and embed itself in the groin of another competitor.

Today, all these years later, Tiffanys has evolved into a DIY store with its latest transformation as a camping & caravan supply shop.

I've done a lot of stuff in my life so far. Lots of activities, doing this and that. Always busy doing. Many times I'd heard the saying "We are human beings not human doings". The more I thought about it, the less I knew what I wanted to do when I grew up. I flitted between childhood, teenager years and my life now. All the big questions. Who am I? Why am I here? Am I living my life's purpose? What is my life purpose? This is the stuff that I used to ridicule the others in the office about when they started banging on about it.

It felt like an internal argument going on inside my head. One side was saying "Pull yourself together, these are crazy thoughts" and the other side was saying "It's time, you took the time, to consider". Which side would win? Am I going crazy? Perhaps I'd had a sugar rush from all that cereal!

Personal development? Personally I couldn't see the point; to me this was just a scam to rip off gullible people. "Gullible" in the dictionary fits like the meat in a sandwich between the two slices of bread either side – F for foolish and H for harebrained.

I nestled down in the bed and thumped the pillow a few times to get the filling where I wanted it and closed my eyes. As I drifted off to sleep I saw the face of the personal development woman on the billboard poster calling my name.

I'm not sure how long I slept but it appears that the internal argument had continued and there was a winner. I woke up thinking about my colleagues who had all paid shedloads for tickets to see this personal development woman.

I had been offered a free ticket.

"You know", I thought, "I might just check it out for myself!"

--X--

My mind drifted back to a time when I was 12, a very vivid time for me when I wanted to be a train driver. I used to play down by the station and as I lay there I could recall the sound of the doors slamming shut, one after the other, along the length of the train before the sound of the whistle and the train pulling away. The station manager, George, agreed that I could travel on the train for free – "just one stop, then come back, be careful how you swap over onto the other platform." I loved it. There was nothing like hearing the slam of the door from the inside. I was on an adventure. An adventure that started by opening the window in the door and hanging my head out all the way; letting the air rush over my face. There was a long, dark, exciting tunnel between the two stops. Life couldn't be any better.

My friend Jack has a constant reminder of those old fashioned doors.

He was rushing for the train one day and just made it as the train pulled away. Unfortunately, he forgot to close the door! The door banged a few times against the train and then there was an almighty clap as the train entered one side of the tunnel and emerged the other side with a newly designed "air conditioned" carriage. To this day, he has a copy of the British Rail fine *and* the discarded door.

Life was less complicated then. Back then I had my whole lifetime ahead of me. Recently, I felt like I'd been going through a long dark tunnel in my life with no light at the end of it.

In my opinion we have lost the magic of that train age. More importantly though, I think, I've lost the magic that was me. Where did he go? Back then, no-one was going to stop me, I had my whole lifetime in front of me with infinite possibilities, I could be whatever I wanted to be. I was only limited by my own imagination. I was going to take on the world and *win* of course. Then someone burst my bubble and said, "Wake up, welcome to reality." I listened to the voice of reason and did the sensible thing; I lowered my aims. Just a little to start with, but then as time went on, each year I would lower the bar of my dreams until I was at the place where I am now. The bar was temporarily raised with my ex-girlfriend, but that relationship bar had now been lowered again.

What if we actually create our own reality? Maybe I allowed someone to burst my bubble. What could have happened if I'd said, "No, this is my reality" and continued with my own hopes and dreams? Maybe we can be masters of our own destiny by being true to ourselves and not going with the crowd?

All these questions were going around in my head. I could have done with some internal peace and quiet right then. No sooner had I had that thought when I saw the piece of paper with the message on it: "You already have what you seek within you."

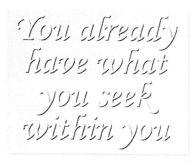

All I had was a stomach full of cereal, a bed full of cornflake crumbs, and a head that felt like grandma had been hitting it with the barbeque tongs! This feels like "the morning after" a good night out. Time to get up out of my pit and do something constructive with my extended weekend.

Over the next few days my mind returned to all of these questions and thoughts, and most of all, back to the statement on the piece of paper. The more I thought, the more I realised that this had to do with finding me. The part of me that never changed. The child within. All my hopes and dreams were bound up in there, I was sure of it.

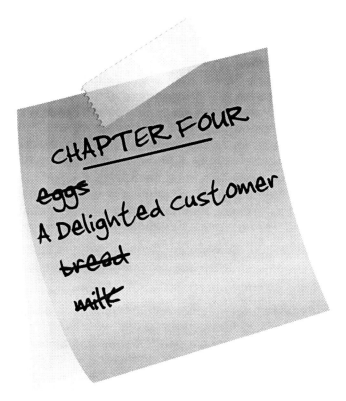

A week went by before I ventured back to the supermarket. This time with no list, no trolley, no basket, just an open mind and open eyes, seeing for the first time how others tend to do their shopping. They have such busy lives. Packed full of so many things that they only shop when they are desperate; some with no time to make a list of what they need, let alone what they want.

I wondered if they dash up and down the aisles throwing things into their "life" trolley in much the same way? Filling until the trolley is so stuffed with "stuff" there's no room for peace anyway? And then head for the checkout as fast as possible. Paying for all this "stuff", knowing that it won't last and that they will need to be back there again soon to do it all over again. Then they will probably have less time than they do now. And if that's not crazy enough, I saw some people with two trolleys doing exactly the same thing only now twice as much stuff costing twice as much but still with no peace.

I wandered back to the place where peace was on the shelf. I watched as many people just walked past it. They were truly blinkered. They just didn't get it.

Then, I spotted a young woman calmly walk towards the CDs. Would she see the peace boxes next to them or be like the others and walk away? To my amazement, she picked up a peace box and put it in her trolley. It was as if she knew that I was watching her, she looked straight at me and smiled. She said, "Hi, my name's Sue, I saw you last week. I wondered if you would be back or if you would be like the others and throw the box away?"

I smiled, and invited her for a coffee. During the next hour I learnt that she was a local university student in her final year. She had led the traditional student life and enjoyed her time but as she spoke I knew that there was something very different about Sue. She had a fun, loving, bubbly character. I could see her as the life and soul of the party and yet there was a deep sense of peace and tranquillity about her.

As we talked together, it was if we had met before; like long lost friends who had been reunited and were just catching up. She had a way of making the conversation flow. Which was a good thing because my confidence had gone; this was the first real conversation I'd had with someone outside of work. No cheesy chat-up lines, no taking over the conversation and making me the centre of attention. Normally, I'm like some deranged peacock trying to show off all my colours in front of a woman. Instead, I listened as this young woman told me how she had seen many people pick up the boxes only to throw them in the bin as soon as they were outside.

"Why don't they get it?" I asked.

Sue said, "It's not their time yet. But," she continued, "The frequency of people who are getting it, is increasing! The awareness is increasing!" Sue continued, "You are the first person I've seen in a while who has 'got it'."

As our conversation continued Sue shared her own experience of finding peace in a box, and the changes it had made to her life over the past year.

She'd been abused as a child and carried some emotional baggage until she discovered a peace box at the supermarket. Sue had been shopping and then noticed another woman in the same aisle as her. When I say noticed her, I don't mean she saw her; it was more of an "experience". Sue described to me that she had a sinking feeling not dissimilar to how you experience turbulence on an aeroplane, when you drop in altitude. As Sue looked around, she saw she was actually standing next to the woman who had abused her as a child.

Her heart pounded as she ran for the exit. Thinking she was a shoplifter a security guard hastily followed her. Once outside Sue sat on the bench and the tears flowed like a river. The Security guard saw this and signalled to the store manager who invited her back into the store and sat her in the restaurant with a coffee. The river of tears continued and through blurred vision her eyes were drawn to aisle 13 and the strange PEACE box section between the CDs and the DVDs.

Both of us had had different journeys separated by 12 months, however, we had arrived at the same place. Sue enquired, "So, how's your week been since you found the message in the peace box?"

"Strange", I replied, and then added "I've done a lot of soul searching but I've got more questions now than answers."

She remarked, "It's interesting the phrases you are using. Have you stopped to consider the words? Words like, 'the life and soul of the party', or 'soul searching questions'?" Sue continued, "What do you think about when you hear to the word soul?"

Until that point I hadn't given it any thought really. Soul, spirit, inner self, the real "me" inside. Yes, I suppose to me it meant the essence of who I am, the child within. The part of me that I've always had, that has never changed even though I've physically grown.

As we sat together Sue shared how we were all triads. "Aren't they a native American Indian Tribe?" I joked. Sue gave me a knowing look and a smack on the arm.

"The word triads," she continued, "describes how we are body, mind and spirit. For us to achieve brilliant results in all areas of our lives we need to engage the whole person."

At that moment a large man walked past us and sat on a table in front of us. On his tray were a coffee and a large cream cake. Sue had however noticed something completely different.

"Take a look at his shopping bags..." she said. As I looked I noticed the contents were mainly diet related products. Sue remarked, "There's a classic example. This man's mind is telling him that he needs to do something about his size, so his body and mind are working together. However, the fact he's now sitting with a large cream cake makes you realise that his spirit isn't in unison. Whatever is going on with the spirit of this real person inside this body is sabotaging his attempt to get a handle on his weight. It's the same with every area of our lives, personal, relationships or work. The vast majority are sabotaging their own happiness, peace and fulfilment in life."

As I took some time to process this Sue smiled at me, knowing that she was just about to give me something that would really get my brain working. "Triads – Native American Indian Tribe" she laughed, shaking her head. "Do you remember hearing that the Native American Indians had an aversion to having their photograph taken because they believed that it took away their soul?"

I nodded as Sue conspiratorially asked, "Was this so wrong after all?" At this point, I started to worry that we were "off with the fairies"!

Sue explained, rather than thinking of physical photography, consider the memory (mental images) we store all the time in our mind. When we think of these images, don't we also experience the emotions attached with the picture too? Whether good or bad experiences the emotional attachment is there. In fact, the stronger the emotion the more focussed and memorable that image becomes. Our emotions have the ability to turn up the intensity of the volume, brightness, colour and contrast of any given memory picture.

On a physical level we know about the flight or fight response; if people find themselves in either stress or danger the body will secrete the hormone adrenalin which will raise the blood pressure. That then produces a rapid heartbeat and in general, pushes the body's alarm bell notifying all the systems to be on red alert.

Sue noticed that I was deep in thought and asked me to explain. My mind had gone back to being 13 years old and being bullied after school each night as I walked the 15-minute distance from the school gates to my home. A group of lads would hide in different places each night and would jump out on me and fight me. I never knew where the attack would happen only that it *would* happen.

Sue replied, "There's an example of what I mean. The memory is there, the emotion is there, but what was the effect on you – the child within? Even now, what is the effect on you as a result of that situation after all these years?"

"It's like a time-bubble that has sealed everything in it about you and that section of your life. What if all the sections of you to date have been stored in these time bubbles and if they have, where would they be stored?" Sue was in full flow now. "My imagination says that this time-bubble store looks like bubble wrap with rows upon rows of these bubbles."

"Is this where I've lost 'me'?" I asked. "In bubbles that store my memories and all my emotions. All my energy, my passion and my drive sealed together?

"Is this why my enthusiasm to take on the world has diminished and my 'that will do' mentality has started to creep into my thoughts and actions?"

Sue nodded knowingly, "Correct!"

At this point, she looked at her watch and said she had to leave and that she would see me again next week. As she left she reminded me to pick up my box of peace for this week. After Sue had gone the whole experience of meeting her left me with a stronger sense of peace.

As I looked at the peace in a box shelf all the boxes looked the same to me. I wondered, how I would know which one to get, after all what would be the sense in picking up another one that has the message "You already have what you seek within you." In the end I picked up a box and went to the checkout.

On my journey home every set of lights I approached seemed to be on red. Normally after the second set I would be fuming as the red mist descends and patience goes out of the car window. This time was different though. I sat thinking about the sequence of the lights: Red, Red & Amber and Green.

I related this to what Sue had said about us being a triad. *"For us to achieve brilliant results in all areas of our lives we need to engage the whole person."*

Body, mind and spirit.

RED (Body only) – You'll probably find this hard to believe I'm sure, but sometimes I've been accused of being "shallow"! I suppose this would be when I've been chasing a woman based purely on looks alone. I do have a tick list of what I'm looking for, but don't we all build a picture of our ideal partner? I want a beautiful woman around my age who is shorter in height than me, who has long hair and a good figure.

RED & AMBER (Body & Mind) – This isn't just about looks though.

This same woman must have a confident attitude and know what she wants out of life. She will have a determination to make things happen and be willing to accept responsibility for her own actions. This is about the meeting and joining together of minds as much as it is about bodies.

GREEN (Body, Mind & Spirit) - This is the final part to be added. When the spirit is united with the body & mind is when the lights are "turned on" in the relationship. The giving of "you"; the real you inside to someone else. Of allowing yourself to be vulnerable but having faith in your partner that they will be there for you. They are your support, your safety net. Knowing that if all else fails, you can rest assured that they will be there for you. This is probably better known by the expressions "waiting to exhale" or "having a soft place to land". Green most definitely means GO!

It was one of those "light bulb" moments that we all have from time to time; it seems so obvious, so simple, so why haven't I thought about it before? When I actually thought about it, the best times of my life were when I did fully engage Body, Mind and Spirit simultaneously.

It's like when you meet someone for the first time and you instantly have a good level of rapport. This is all down to the level of connection between you. Body; body & mind; or all three, body, mind and spirit.

Like a jigsaw piece with either one, two or three interlocking parts. The more connections, the more secure that piece is in the whole puzzle.

The strongest intimacy I've felt has been when we have both grown and developed the relationship by the joining together of two people at all levels, body, mind and spirit simultaneously.

My thoughts were broken as the lights changed and I moved again, strangely calmer now.

Jim Parkes

My eyes scanned the interior of the car as I waited at the next set of traffic lights. I looked at the GPS (global positioning system) unit sitting on my dashboard that was switched off. I'm one of the worst people for directions and I would not be without this friend in the car these days.

My reputation for always being late stems from my inability to navigate myself out of a paper bag, let alone around the streets. This lateness is now a trademark. There is "fashionably late" and then there's me! I can no longer blame this on my "directional dysfunction" as I now have the technology.

The macro-technology behind this small piece of kit on my dashboard is incredible. There are 24 "celestial bodies" more commonly known as orbiting satellites constantly travelling around this planet of ours. It only takes three of those to pinpoint exactly where we are using longitude, latitude and altitude. None of this will work however until I push the button on the receiver in the car. As soon as I do the LED display lights up and I'm presented with a number of choices.

What is my starting location? What is my final destination? As soon as I give the information all three satellites work together in synergy and determine my starting position and my final destination and the macro-technology plots the route. I don't need to worry how the system works, I just need to know that it does and it will guide me every single step along the way. Even if I should move off course it will continue to guide me and steer me back on track.

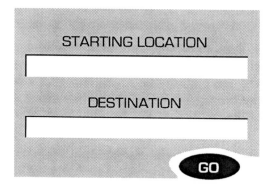

There are further choices I can make with this system; longest or scenic route, shortest route, avoiding traffic hot spots etc. This allows me to control the journey even if I don't know the route that I should take. This guidance will talk me through my journey as I travel. It will also show me the way on the visual display, which allows me to zoom in and out to give me an overall perspective of my route. It doesn't matter whether it's light or dark, clear or pea soup fog – my guidance system will always steer me towards my destination.

After 5 years of living 2 miles from the supermarket even I don't need celestial assistance to get home.

Comfortably sitting at home I opened the peace box and inside was another message that simply read "Push The Button". Looking at these words and into the flames of the fire I allowed my thoughts to drift off and I found myself thinking more about the GPS unit and the three satellites of Body, Mind and Spirit. If I could find the internal button and push it, could I live my life on a consistent basis engaging all three micro-technologies –

body, mind and spirit? Could I proactively live my life like this? And if I did, what difference would it make?

As my eyes grew heavier I drifted off to sleep. I usually have the strangest dreams and tonight was no exception. It must have been the thought of the traffic light colours because there was a sort of a theme, albeit a dreamy theme of colours, in fact all the colours of the rainbow. Rainbow, "paint the whole world with a RAINBOW..."

If you're of a certain age you'll recognise these as the words to the theme tune of the 1970s children's TV programme Rainbow. The long suffering and much-loved Geoffrey had to try to control the three characters Zippy, George and Bungle.

If you missed this wonderful piece of children's TV history then here is a brief character identification. Zippy was the mouthy one, who was always up to mischief and also thinking about sweets and cake (Body). George was the shy, pink hippo who always tried to assist Bungle to keep Zippy on the right path (Spirit). And finally Bungle, he was the big bear who was the one with rational thought and would reprimand Zippy on a regular basis (Mind).

From there I dreamed of a beautiful rainbow, which I was able to step onto and walk up, like a flight of stairs. By now you are probably thinking I had taken some illicit substances, but no, this is typical of my dreams! As I walked up the rainbow I started to sing *"Somewhere over the rainbow way up high, there's a land that I've heard of once in a lullaby. Somewhere over the rainbow skies are blue, and the dreams that you dare to dream, really do come true."*

After a number of blissful hours rest I woke with the phrase "the dreams that you dare to dream, really do come true."

What if I dare?

What if I push my internal button and get my three internal satellites to work together to achieve a desired goal or destination point in my life? Just enter my starting point and destination point and let the satellites do the guidance. What if all the coincidences and chance

meetings in my life were me actually being guided from within?

As I drove to work the next day I noticed that the phrase on the billboard advert had been changed to: "What would you do today if you knew that you couldn't fail?" I smiled and sang, "Somewhere over the rainbow ... The dreams that you dare to dream, really do come true."

What does all this mean? And what does this have to do with peace? And where is the button for me to push? Maybe Sue will understand my ramblings and explain more to me. Or will she think I've gone crazy when I see her that evening in the supermarket? I hoped she would come. These thoughts were taking me over, and I needed some answers.

--X--

I arrived early at the supermarket and decided I would do my new-found hobby of watching to see if anyone else would pick up a peace box.

I got really excited for a moment when I saw a crowd of people all gathered around the peace on the shelf. At first I thought it was just a family choosing that spot to have a discussion but as I moved closer I could hear that they were talking about peace. They were saying that this is what is missing in each and every person's life and how the world would be a better place if every one had some peace in their lives.

They did a lot of talking about peace, they even picked up some of the boxes off the shelf, passed them around and all were in awe of this precious commodity. They handled the boxes with care, knowing that the contents were so precious. Then at the end of their meeting, they all dutifully returned the boxes to the shelf and walked away saying to each other, "See you next week."

What were they doing? They had peace within their grasp but didn't take it. Just as if they had been given a gift, and after saying "thank you" walking away without it. How bizarre. If only one person had taken a box to the checkout they would have seen it was free.

At that moment I grabbed a peace box and put it into the shopping trolley of the leader of the group without being seen. I followed from a distance like some private investigator on a surveillance mission. Up and down the aisles this man continued his shopping and all the time I was hovering just a few feet away wishing he would head towards the checkout and see that peace is free of charge. My mind raced around wondering what his reaction would be when he finally had his eyes opened.

At that point Sue tapped me on the shoulder smiled and said, "Isn't that interesting?" and guided me away from my mark. I wanted to know what would happen to this "peace man" but she insisted I should, "leave him alone, he will get it if he's ready". She was more concerned about me.

We sat down and she asked me about my week. I explained about the GPS thoughts and also my crazy dream and fascination with Rainbow. She listened without passing judgement. In fact there was no reaction on her face at all.

"This is exciting" she said, "You are very receptive at the moment and I'm glad you picked up on the macro / micro technology aspect as that is one of the keys to peace."

--X--

Over the next couple of hours this perceptive young woman asked many questions and opened my eyes further. I can only give you the layperson's viewpoint but I'm sure you'll know more about this than I do. So here goes, from a macro level: the satellites are orbiting outside of the gravitational forces that affect us on the planet surface. Of course they are operating within what we loosely refer to as space. Planet earth is the tiniest dot when you consider the concept of space.

Take one of its many phenomena, that of black holes. A black hole, contrary to the normal use of the word *hole*, is actually full of matter that has been sucked inside. This vast outer space has holes, but they are full "wholes". As stars collapse their matter can be sucked into a black hole whose pull takes everything inside and from which nothing can escape, not even light travelling at 186,000 miles per second.

"Now", she said, "Let's zoom back into our earth."

There's no difference once you travel back to earth, the table we are sitting at, although it looks solid, when viewed under a microscope you'd see lots of space in between the atoms of matter. This is true of everything in the world around us.

Just like the analogy with the GPS unit this macro level order of outer-space applies to the inner-space of the three internal satellites of our PPS™ (Personal Positioning System™). As you know, the GPS system requires all three satellites to be aligned to guide you. Your personal 3 satellites are Body, Mind and Spirit, they too need to be aligned. They are your PPS (Personal Positioning System™).

She took each one in turn and gave me examples.

# BODY

We all know the feelings we have when at times our bodies get blockages; how about having a blocked nose or sinuses when you have a cold? Or the discomfort of the mother as her internal organs are moved around to accommodate a growing baby during pregnancy? So even the very nature of our bodies has inbuilt space to breathe and we know the feeling of discomfort when that space is restricted.

Zoom in at greater magnification to the very building block of life itself. The DNA molecule, the actual digital code of life contains two strands wrapped around each other in a spiral or helix. When you look at this structure you can't help but notice the space that's encompassed by the chain.

There are many illustrations she made, but I know by now you can see the concept of the space within us.

# MIND

You may have been told that the majority of us use between 1% and 1.6% of our brain. But what is the difference between the brain and the mind? She made it simple for me: the brain is like computer hardware and our mind is the software that runs on it. Some of us run higher (faster) versions than others but we all in general have the same hardware available. Even people we consider as being geniuses only use a small percentage of their brain capability. The expression that someone has an "open mind" implies there is space to consider alternative options. An openness to evaluate, space is available to turn things over, upside down and view from different angles. This is not possible with a closed mind.

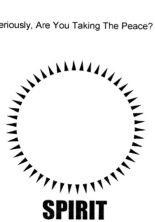

# SPIRIT

We looked at the Macro version of the universe before looking internally. Sue asked me to recall a memory of any of the total eclipses that had happened. The eclipse in 1999 was still fresh in my thoughts and the whole experience was very clear in my mind. I remembered that everyone in our office went outside to see it, like a primeval ritual of man's worship of the sun god. High-powered and respected business people, humble database administrators (like me) and the office junior stood side by side in this great levelling experience. Some wearing bizarre eye protection cardboard glasses given away free in the tabloid press, others with pencils pushing holes in cardboard to create a pin-hole to reflect an image of the sun onto another surface. And yes, of course, the office idiot who says, "I can look at it, I won't go blind".

As the moments passed the tension, or boredom, built depending on whom you spoke to at any given time. Then it happened. The sky started to get darker, as if it was just about to rain. Then it got darker, as if dusk was falling. And then darker. There was stillness.

I distinctly remember noticing that the birds stopped singing and a bee flew past me, his flight pattern was affected, no straight "bee-line" for him at that moment. Then I heard gasps – the solar corona. The very hot and thin gas around the sun is usually invisible as the solar disc is far brighter. But when the moon moved to be in total alignment with the sun, the solar corona was revealed.

The moon started to pass over the sun and we saw the glimpse of the far side of the sun. It was breathtaking. The "diamond ring". This was so beautiful to see, the world stood by to experience such an amazing sight. Every TV channel carried the pictures.

She remarked, "That was a stunning time for us all. Now let's relate that to our spirit. On a micro spirit level that experience happens each and every day as we wake. We choose how we will experience it, do we embrace it as we come out of the darkness of sleep and see the new day as the next corona in our life, or do we turn over and wish we could have another hour in bed? As with the macro level the diamond ring effect is just a passing moment, and then it's gone. It's the same when we awake. The choice we make at that precise moment will have an affect on how we perceive our whole day. As with the physical, once observed and recorded, the playback can be re-shown time after time.

"As we go through our day we can re-capture and replay that moment as often as we wish. In fact, by constantly replaying this experience there will be a number of results. Our lives start to exhibit a calmness and stillness that others will pick up on. They may not know what it is, but they will sense there is something different about you. You will emit peace and tranquillity. This will be visible to those who are tuned into this frequency and vision; they may even see your corona. On a micro level this is usually called seeing someone's aura. The dictionary describes an aura as an effect or a feeling produced by a person or place.

"This aura will draw others towards you like a magnet. This is your energy field, like a primitive desire to connect with the source of this peace. This part relates directly to the rainbow colours that you saw in your dream. Ever wondered why when you see a rainbow your eyes are compelled to look for the full arc of this natural occurrence? There it is again; the strong connection with the macro and the micro."

This talk of auras was getting too philosophical and spiritual for me. I wanted some practical answers. "This is really interesting," I said, "But how do I push the button on my PPS?" Seeing my impatience, she smiled and then gave me the Push The Button Technique™.

# PUSH THE BUTTON TECHNIQUE™

Not surprisingly, this technique has three bits, each of which is as important as the other. Sue warned me that there is a level of commitment required and this should not be underestimated. As with anything new at first, it seems impossible for us to do, however by making a commitment to do this for 30 days we create a new habit. Pushing the button through this initial pain barrier will make the difference.

---

### Start your day earlier

Whatever time you get up at the moment, set the alarm 20 minutes earlier. Don't spend that extra time extending your usual morning tasks, this 20 minutes is about preparing you for the day ahead. Think about the outcome you want from that day. Imagine you are now back home after that day is over and you are reflecting over it. What will be the tangible and intangible things that you want to achieve today? What will confirm that this day has been beneficial to you? Prepare yourself emotionally and also prepare the child within. What do you want from today?

### Take a lunch break

Whilst this is not the accepted norm in today's working environment, it's important to have 20 minutes to yourself during the course of a day. Use time management techniques to structure your day to ensure that you have some quality time for re-aligning your satellites. Consider your thoughts and emotions from this morning's 20 minutes, how is your day lining up? Are you still on track, if not, what can you do this afternoon to address that?

---

> **At the end of the day**
>
> Take a final 20 minutes at the end of your day to review how close your initial thoughts were to the reality of the actual day. Capture your thoughts, emotions and how the day was for you internally. Write these in a daily journal.

"I don't have an hour each day to do all that", I complained. Sue suggested that I needed to re-think my priorities and make the time to do it. She said that I could build this up over the next 30 days. If I started with just five minutes per section per day for the first week, then ten minutes the 2nd week, 15 minutes the 3rd week, I would be ready by the 4th week to be at 20 minutes per session.

| End of Week | Time spent pushing the button |
|---|---|
| Week 1 | 1 hour 45 minutes |
| Week 2 | 3 hours 30 minutes |
| Week 3 | 5 hours 15 minutes |
| Week 4 | 7 hours |
| **Month Total** | **17 hours 30 minutes** |

"Fantastic," I said, "Now I have something I can physically do over the next seven days." I enjoy looking at and throwing new ideas and concepts around but I also like to have a pragmatic approach to try out these ideas in a practical way.

I made the commitment that for the next seven days I would do three sessions per day each lasting five minutes as instructed and I would discuss this at our next meeting in the supermarket. After all, how hard could it be to take five minutes out three times a day?

Seeing that I was feeling more comfortable she said two words to me. "Bubble wrap!"

"Yes, bubble wrap, I love it!" I said. "There's nothing quite like it, I can't describe the pleasure I get when I can sit there and pop the bubbles."

Talking of the child within, I wish bubble wrap had been around when I was a kid. Whether I pop the bubbles individually or twist a whole section and have a multiple-popping time, I love it! It ought to be sold as Stress Management relief. My head was swivelling, scanning the supermarket to see if I could see any to appease my desire.

Sue brought my attention back by explaining the time-bubble theory she had mentioned and about the bubble store. So many people do lose themselves in this way. These bubbles or pockets are filled with memories, emotions and also a part of them is in there too. It is only a minute part so as not to be missed on a daily basis. But the compound effect is staggering, as these bubbles also encapsulate their energy and enthusiasm. At the start we are full of vitality and energy and over time this leaks out into the bubbles until we are left with precious little to give out any more.

It's like having a hole in a bucket; when the bucket is full it's not that great a problem, over time the bucket will empty.

The time-bubbles affect us all; the only difference is the size of bubble. When someone goes through the "burn out" stage, obviously, the bubbles were large. Left unchecked, the time bubbles can drain your spirit until there's nothing much left. As we are triads, of course this will have a knock-on effect to both the body and also the mind. Physical and mental breakdowns are the natural progression and conventional medical treatments will look to deal with the effects but will not address the cause, that of a spiritual draining of the individual.

"What can be done about this?" I asked.

"A very simple solution" she replied, "Just the same as you enjoy popping bubble wrap then if these time bubbles are burst all the memories, emotions, energy, passion and the minute part of yourself is released back into your spirit and the 'bucket starts to fill up again.' It's like putting the charge back into drained batteries, increasing their energy.

"When we go on holiday it's sometimes referred to as recharging. Again, that's normally only completed on a physical and mental level; if you remember when you were a kid I bet you had a bike, or knew someone that had one with lights that were powered by a dynamo?"

"Oh yes, I'd forgot about those", I said. Looking back now it seems crazy that the lights were powered only when the wheels were turning. Waiting at traffic lights, something I seemed to have done all my life, the bike lights would go out!

"Well", she said, "That's how it is when you go away to charge your batteries but only end up recharging your body and mind. We miss out the most important part – recharging the spirit."

"Why do we allow these bubbles to exist in the first place?" I wanted to know.

"Ironically, this is our mind's defence system. Although we are triads we do have to make the conscious decision to push the button on our receiver. This will make the connection so that each individual 'satellite' knows that we want the three to start to work together. Their individual normal operation is to look after themselves and not work as a team. When we power up our PPS™ surprisingly, it's our spirit that is the dominant one because it's our spirit that uses our body and mind.

"To give an illustration, a car has the potential of carrying us on a journey. It has the power in the engine for movement. However, until we take some actions the car's not going anywhere. It's our spirit that directs the action of the body and mind and not the other way around. The majority of people, most of the time, live their lives like the old saying 'the tail wagging the dog'.

"Let me give you an example, someone suffers a traumatic experience. The mind constructs the outer case of the bubble and then sucks into that the memory of that experience. So we now have a memory bubble. But that's not all that is in there. Also, the associated emotional response is encapsulated. So too is the 'effect of' those emotions on the 'child within'. We talk of people losing, self–confidence, self–worth. If they have lost it, where is it? This lost or damaged spirit is also included in the bubble. This is the mind trying to protect the remainder of itself and also of the spirit, and, depending on the severity of traumatic experience; the body and mind could also go into shock as a means of self-preservation.

"This bubble making process can take a considerable amount of time to complete. Once complete, the mind will put the time-bubble away into the bubble store and will attempt to resume normal functioning. This is what is generally referred to as 'bottling up' the emotions or 'keeping the lid' on things. What people don't realise is that they are weakening their spirit every time a new bubble is created. If we burst the bubbles and release all that latent pressure, a full and complete healing can take place in body, mind and spirit. It's the reverse of a builders' spirit level, if that loses its bubble, it's useless. If however, we burst our internal bubbles we can become more than we ever dare to dream. Because the dreams that we dare to dream *do* come true.

"It must be stressed at this time that attempting to burst these bubbles as a DIY job is a potentially dangerous activity. As with the body, if a blister is burst and not taken care of, infections can set in. In the same way, if the spirit is not dealt with in a professional way, infection can be caused and the situation is worsened rather than there being healing. Whilst bearing that in mind, when these bubbles are burst the peace that ensues is sheer bliss and the spirit regains its strength and energy and once more is ready to rise up like a phoenix from the ashes."

As Sue talked, I found myself getting more tired and although this was an interesting discussion, my mind was shutting up shop for the evening. I was always astonished at the energy of this woman. I'd put that down to her bubbly character but after listening that night I could now see where she got her energy. She's obviously recognised her spirit bubbles and has dealt with them returning the energy back to its source.

We said our goodbyes and I made my way over to aisle 13 to pick up my next peace in a box, knowing this time whichever box I picked up from the shelf would be the right one for me. That the message inside would be the one I should have. The belief in my PPS™ unit was real, I'd pushed the button and had confidence that I was being internally guided. That, my friends, is an incredible feeling that you have to experience yourself.

I'd heard the expression fake it until you make it many times and it's never sat well with me. I never wanted to be false with others. There's the famous quote from Shakespeare's Hamlet, "This above all: to thyself be true, for it must follow as dost the night the day, that canst not then be false to any man." With my PPS™ operational, I speak with truth and integrity and I know that I am being guided internally.

At home I sat down and started to mull over the conversation I'd just had. My eyes were heavy and closing and I knew that I'd a busy day at work ahead of me so I dragged myself to bed and within seconds I was fast asleep.

I woke before the alarm went off, which was handy, as I needed to be up five minutes earlier than normal to start my week of Push The Button Technique™.

Preparing for the day ahead was fun. I decided what I wanted the outcome to be, thought about the tangible and intangible things I wanted and prepared myself emotionally for the day. Just taking 5 minutes to focus on what I wanted from this day. When I get to work, my bosses are clear what they want from me, now it's time that I know what *my* agenda is too for the whole of my day.

After that, I continued my daily routine. As I sat eating breakfast, I reached over and picked up the peace box from last night. Knowing that this message was the right one for me I opened the box to find this message: "Life is not like a box of chocolates... it's like a piece of Swiss cheese." What the??!!

*Life is not like a box of chocolates*

*It's like a piece of Swiss Cheese*

I was expecting another deep meaningful message with lots of rich undertones for me to consider for the next seven days, instead I have a mental picture of Tom Hanks as Forrest Gump and the theme music to Wallace & Gromit going through my head, with the voice of Peter Sallis saying, "No cheese, Gromit?"

Technically I suppose I should be thinking about Wensleydale if I'm picturing Wallace & Gromit but the peace box especially said Swiss cheese. I grabbed my jacket on the way out the door as these November mornings are definitely turning colder. There was a strong smell of potassium nitrate, charcoal and sulphur in the air that morning after all the fireworks, or should I say explosions, that were going off as I went to sleep. It was like being on a battlefield with shells exploding all around me.

Each year, my neighbours wage war against each other to see who can light up the most sky and make the biggest noise. Once this battle is concluded detailed strategic planning goes on well into the November evenings behind closed curtains, to see if it's possible to fit more Christmas lights and scenes on the house, garden walls, fences, tree, telegraph poles etc., than last year.

I knew that today was going to be a difficult day at work; this was tempered throughout the morning by hearing in my head, "No cheese Gromit?" At one point the people around me thought I'd lost the plot as I said this out loud.

Normally, I would grab a sandwich from the canteen and continue my work as a DBA (Database Administrator) within the IT department of a large company. Today I knew that I had to fit in my five minutes PTBT (Push The Button Technique™) Life is full of acronyms isn't it? I decided to take a walk in the park and watch the world go by for a few minutes, then I reviewed my morning and re-assessed and realigned my PPS™ ready for the afternoon.

I completed my work and was out of that place by 6pm satisfied that I had achieved my objectives for that day. Day two started as positively as the previous day, however, things overtook me and I was back in headless chicken mode before the end of that day. I did complete my end of day review by taking ten minutes rather than five to make up for missing lunchtime.

It was at that time that I realised what Sue said was true; I should not underestimate the commitment I was to make. I was determined not to fail and I really wanted to see this through. The rest of the week I was on track and surprisingly I was wishing I could take more than the 5 minutes at times, but this too was part of the discipline of this technique.

Sue said that I should continue with the 30 day challenge and she would encourage me by email but I was not to respond, just to take the message and consider what it meant to me. The content of the first email is shown below.

# SWISS CHEESE

An easy way to think about this is that in a perfect world we resemble something that looks like Swiss cheese in our PPS™ (body, mind and spirit). It's like looking at a piece of Emmental; its holes give it its distinct appearance and character. As the cheese is being fermented, propimic acid is produced which causes carbon dioxide to form inside the body of the cheese. Until the rind is formed this gas is released through the cheese itself. When the rind is formed there is no place for the gas to dissipate, as a result bubbles appear and burst leaving the holes in the cheese.

As we are physically formed within the womb we are surrounded by fluid to assist growth and development. Peace is flowing through the developing body, mind and spirit of the embryo during the early stages until the time when its flow is restricted because of the physical human form. From this time forward, peace bubbles up and burst inside body, mind and spirit creating holes, and as we discussed earlier, like a black hole in space, these suck the peace back inside themselves and there it stays until we notice a hole within ourselves.

Unfortunately, many people have mistakenly seen these holes as a sign of lack, need or even want that are aching to be filled. From an early age we start to replace the peace in these internal holes with material things such as sweets, chocolate & toys, to find they only satisfy us for a time. If we had left the space we would have found that we would remain satisfied and peace-full. We actually forced out the peace from the hole as we stuffed in the possessions. The word Possessions is used here in the widest possible meaning.

I'm sure you have heard of someone who has lost a life partner after many years. Sometimes they lose the will to live themselves. Why? Because that relationship filled the partner's very being, they had given all of their inner space over to the other person and when that person leaves, they leave a vacuum behind instead of the individual's own inner peace.

We replace our own inner peace constantly throughout our whole lifetime until one day we realise that there is no peace in our lives at all and that we are always chasing the "next thing".

Here is the problem; even if we had some peace we wouldn't be able to sustain it because we have nowhere to put it permanently. Isn't it ironic that we call the 18" of space around us personal space and that we are uncomfortable if someone enters that space without our permission, but we will gladly fill all the space inside of ourselves without a second thought?

Even our own language offers us clues. Let's have a look at an anagram and how you would phonetically pronounce the resultant word after you re-arrange the letters. The initial word is SPACE, re-arranging the letters give PEASC (peace). If you want more peace in your life create more space within your body, mind and spirit.

We talk about people being a "free spirit" or being "light-hearted". If your spirit looks like a piece of Swiss cheese – wouldn't you be light and have the ability to float above the clouds to where there is always blue sky?

The Push the Button Technique™ is an excellent tool to use to start to empty some of the junk out of our lives. It acts as a pilot hole drilled in the centre of a cluttered hole. Imagine it's the hole drilled for a stick of dynamite to be placed in. It's the pre-cursor to the main removal and subsequent refilling of that hole with peace again, thereby giving us all more space, more room to breathe, relax and regenerate our own energy.

Yours peacefully

Sue

Jim Parkes

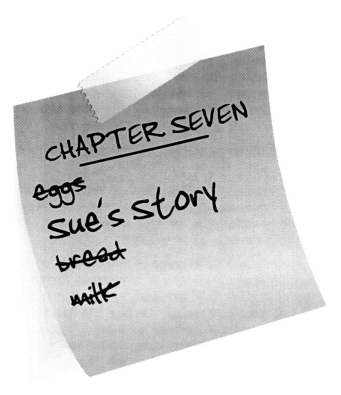

As we sat together that following Monday in the coffee shop, Sue shared with me more of her own story. A story of being in a dark place as a child and feeling totally alone. When she thought things couldn't get any worse, they did. She felt trapped in a pit with no means of an escape.

This incredible woman had lived through these horrors. Yet it was hard to grasp as Sue was so at peace as she retold the story to me. Many times during the conversation I had wanted to say something, but I decided to give Sue the space and the time to share her story with me.

What follows is Sue's account as we sat drinking coffee together.

*I grew up as part of a close family, Mom, Dad and my brother Paul who was three years younger than me. I was a very happy child, I loved my primary school, all my friends and the teachers were great.*

*Things weren't so nice at home as Mom had a rough time with my Dad, there were lots of arguments. Mom used to say, "It's Okay, I like the making up after, all the flowers and your dad treats me like a princess." Many times Mom would be covered in bruises but that was normal family life in our house. There were occasions when Dad took Mom for meals to say "sorry" and when he did my Aunty (my Dad's sister) would baby-sit. We used to look forward to seeing her, she was good fun. When it was time for bed she would chase us up into our separate bedrooms and tickle us. She'd then read a story to my brother and settle him down and then come in and read me a story too.*

For my ninth birthday I wanted a bike, this caused a big argument because I heard Dad shouting that they hadn't got the money. I blamed myself for this row, if I hadn't asked for a bike, it wouldn't have happened. In the end I had some really cool roller-skates, you know, the inline type, none of my friends had these so I was very popular as they all wanted to try them out.

Dad organised another "sorry meal" out for him and Mom and Aunty came around to look after us. We knew the routine; Mom and Dad could never understand why we did not complain when Aunty said it was time for bed as we normally tried to drag out bedtime to get an extra five or ten minutes.

On this occasion, when Aunty had settled Paul down and she came to my room, instead of tickling me she hugged me and stroked my long blonde hair and said that I was growing up now and that we were going to play some new special games together. But these were so special that I wasn't to tell anyone else about them, and, if I did, she wouldn't come to see me again. Normally she would sit on the bed next to me but this time was different, this time she lay on the bed with me and started to touch me under my nightie. I didn't understand the games, I just knew that they didn't seem right to me. Normally she would give me a kiss on the cheek, now she was kissing and touching me everywhere.

These special games continued for 18 months. Each time the front door opened and she was there, I used to feel physically sick but I couldn't say anything to anyone because she had told me that if I did, the police would take me away and I wouldn't see Mom, Dad or Paul ever again.

I used to think that I was a bad girl and that this was all my fault, like most of the rows that Mom and Dad had. I used to think that I must be a really bad girl to have caused all these rows and for Mom to be so bruised and hurt all the time. It was all my fault.

This bright, bubbly girl changed into a sad frightened girl. I withdrew into myself. No one knew the hell I was going through and I couldn't tell anyone, especially, the ones I loved the most, or they would be taken from me.

I lost most of my friends, except Sadie, my one special friend; but I couldn't take the chance telling her.

One day I went around Sadie's house to play. As I rang the door bell, the door flung open and Sadie pushed past me saying "Come on!"

As I rushed to catch her up her face was so angry, I said, "What's the matter?" There was no answer. Her paced quickened as we entered the park. She headed straight for the swings, within seconds she was almost as high as the bar. I was scared that she was going to fall off! I shouted "What's the matter?" Sadie let her swing naturally slow down enough for her to jump off. She ran as fast as she could to the climbing frame. Within seconds she was sitting at the top swinging her feet.

I couldn't stand heights, but slowly I started to climb up. "Don't look down, don't look down", I kept saying to myself. Every step I took I was getting more scared, my heart was pounding now. But my friend needed me, and I wasn't going to let her down. Finally, I was sitting at the top of the frame next to Sadie. My knuckles were turning white as I gripped the bars tightly. I couldn't let Sadie see how scared I was. "What's the matter?" I said.

*Sadie's tear drenched face turned to me and said "My Dad started to touch me down there." She cried. "I just had to get out of the house, I don't know what to do?" Suddenly, the fear of heights left me, I let go of the bars and gave Sadie a hug. We both cried, I then shared with her about what had been happened to me. There, on the top of the climbing frame, we made a promise to look after each other. Whatever happened we had a friend we could trust.*

"Want another top up?" Sue asked me.

"Yes, but it's my turn" I replied.

"No, problem, you can get the next one," and with that Sue walked over to the counter. The sounds of the freshly brewed coffee machine were drowned out by the thoughts that went through my mind. Now there were two abused girls trying to help each other.

Sue smiled as she put a fresh hot cup of black coffee in front of me. As she sat down she continued...

*Sadie and I did so much growing up together. When we changed schools, we both went to the same high school and learned to live with what was going on at home because now we had each other. That seemed to make it okay.*

*One day I was angry when I went to school, I said to Sadie, "That's it, I've had enough of this, this is where it stops - right now!" Earlier that week, we had seen a video at school in our PSHE lesson (Personal, Health and Social Education). What was happening to us both was not our fault.*

*"Are you coming?" I asked Sadie.*

"Where?" she replied.

"I'm going to see the school counsellor, are you coming?" Two twelve year olds walking down the corridor to Mrs Jones' room.

"Hello girls, can I help you?"

Just six words: Hello girls, can I help you...

The answer to those words changed our lives for the better.

Mrs Jones was wonderful! She listened to us both as we told of the situations that were happening at home. Over the coming days and weeks there were people to talk to, forms that had to be filled in, more people to see, but through it all Mrs Jones stood by us every step of the way.

We didn't know that there were so many people out there who were just waiting to help us. All we had to do was ask. As children we didn't know that we had a choice. We thought this is how it is and this is how it will stay. What a tragedy!

Sadie and I had counselling through the rest of our time at school to deal with the trauma but together we rebuilt the pieces of our shattered lives. We both went on to get good grades at school and at sixth form and then went off to university. Without Mrs Jones' help during that period of growing up I hate to think of where we would be today.

I had not seen my Aunt from that time until I felt her presence in the supermarket 12 months ago. That felt like I was free-falling down a long and dark tunnel gathering speed as I fell – all the fear came rushing back *and my whole body felt like it was tearing open all the old wounds again.*

*With the aid of the "peace boxes" I have been able to revisit my childhood and restore the peace into my spirit. So what you see today is the real Sue, the whole Sue, the me as I really should be.*

With that, Sue smiled, stood up and came over to me and gave me a hug. As she moved away, I noticed that her coffee cup was now next to mine. "Get the coffees in" she said with a cheeky smile.

The aroma was delightful as the man freshly brewed two more coffees. I turned around to catch a glimpse of Sue as she sat peacefully at the table. She sensed my gaze and smiled at me.

As I returned to the table Sue remarked, "The tragedy now is that there are many adults who feel they have no choice. They are stuck in a certain place, whether that be an abusive relationship, a job they hate or just in a situation they don't want to be in. They don't see that there are many people out there waiting to help them. All they need to do is ask. Their current circumstances are just one of the many options available to them. There are other choices."

"Do you mean like the old saying, can't see the wood for the trees?" I asked.

Sue explained, "Yes, that's exactly the point. They need to take a break away from that constant fight or flight battle. They need to employ the Push The Button Technique™ to provide that space. Because it's in that space that the choices will reveal themselves."

As we left the coffee shop Sue reminded me to keep the journal updated on a regular basis as this would be an excellent resource to reflect on. What follows is a copy of my 30 day journal.

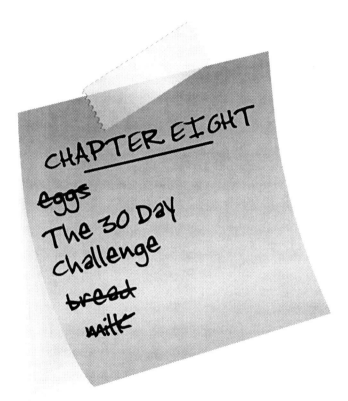

CHAPTER EIGHT

~~eggs~~
The 30 Day Challenge

~~bread~~

~~milk~~

# MY JOURNAL - WEEK 1

This was a real challenge to start off with; it appeared to be such an easy task, to just take five minutes out, three times a day to make a change in my life. But it was tough to condition my body, mind and spirit to actually do it.

It was easy to say, "It's only five minutes, what could I possibly achieve in such a short space of time? I'll leave it and do it later."

But on the other hand, having the discipline to say, "That's it, the five minutes is up," was a challenge too!

I felt like there wasn't enough time to do anything of worth. It did show me the importance of how precious time is and that I needed to focus all of my attention on the task, as I couldn't afford to let my mind wander for a moment or the time would have been wasted.

This may sound strange but it taught me that I (my spirit) could control what my mind was to think about during that time, in contrast to the remainder of my day where I seem to have loads of tasks, activities, thoughts all screaming around in my head for my urgent attention at the same time. It appears that most of the time my mind is in control of me rather than the other way around. Like I mentioned earlier about the tail wagging the dog.

This week has shown me that it's about being consistent and persistent rather than trying to make giant steps in the first week of this Push the Button Technique™.

At the end of this first week I was feeling less stressed during the actual sessions. However, I'd be lying if I said my whole life changed from this point, but I think this was a good start.

## MY JOURNAL - WEEK 2

Building on from last week, although I had doubled the time to ten minutes per session, I was still struggling with the lunchtime one, there always seemed to be something that I needed to do. I know it sounds pathetic, surely I could find just ten minutes in the middle of the day to review the morning and focus on the afternoon?

I suppose it was easy to say, "I couldn't do it because of x, y or z" and put the blame onto someone else. In the end, it's down to me. I make my choices, I can't keep saying, "if only this hadn't happened." I have to take responsibility for what I do.

Ultimately, if I continue to blame others for my situation, then I am giving them control over my life, to be mentally bullied by someone else. It's time I stood up and took responsibility and control over my life. Yes, I will still have the boss breathing down my neck, but how I react to that situation is my decision. I can moan and complain about it and be miserable, or I can decide to do this knowing that he can't affect me inside, unless I let him.

In saying that I may be being hard on myself. I only missed two lunchtime sessions, so I don't think that I'm doing too bad with this challenge. When I think about it, to spend just 30 minutes out of 24 hours to plan, re-plan and review is not too onerous a task.

I feel more in control than ever before in my life. My self-esteem, self-worth and purpose have risen to new levels as a direct result of this on-going exercise. I feel more confident and positive about life in general and overall my mood is good.

Do I feel I have more peace in my life? No, I don't. I'm now half way through this programme and I would have expected to feel something. Maybe it's because I'm halfway through it I'm actually feeling less peaceful than I did before I started!

All those thoughts are in my mind as I received my second email from Sue as I continued the challenge.

# HALFWAY POINT

Now is a good time to reflect on where you have come from and where you are going. One of the learning points of this past 15 days is to make you aware how much time our *heads* think they are in control of us. You have reclaimed ground and shown your head that it's your spirit that is in control.

You may be thinking that at the end of week two, you are only doing just 30 minutes out of 24 hours. Remember, this is an excellent start; this is the finest of drills that is penetrating right into centre of the holes that have been cluttered up. The easiest illustration I can give you is that of an acupuncture needle. When you consider the surface area of the tip of the needle in relation to the surface area of a body it is so minute. However, the effects of that needle on the body can be astounding. This 30 minutes a day is also astounding for body, mind and spirit and the next two weeks will show you how special and remarkable you are.

By now you may be feeling a little confused. Yes, you have some order in your life and that has a positive effect on you and how you perceive yourself and the world around you. However, you are probably concerned that there are still only glimpses of a lasting peace; it's like having a jigsaw peace (pun intended), but without the others you can't keep this picture together.

The next two weeks will give you the pieces to complete this puzzle.

For the remaining two weeks you increase the time by five minutes per session per day, therefore week three will be 15 minutes per session and week four will be 20 minutes per session. Continue the activities you have been doing in week two (10 minutes) and in week three add five minutes per session doing this new activity.

## Visualisation

You have been doing this already on a daily basis as you have considered what outcomes you want out of that day. These five minutes are for you to extend that to focus on something further than one day. It may be that you focus on what you desire in a week, one month, three months, next year, or even 5 years time.

How do you want things to be for you?

This can be in one area of your life or all areas. Use your imagination; make the pictures in your mind as vivid and real as you can. Who is with you? What are they doing? Your unconscious mind will work with the pictures you keep feeding it. If you feed it good things, good things will come to you. Feed it rubbish, rubbish will come to you. It's like the old computer saying "garbage in... garbage out".

Whatever you give your unconscious to think about, it will work to bring those things into existence for you.

If you currently watch or listen to the news before you go to bed, stop this for the next two weeks. Don't feed your unconscious mind on these negative images. If possible, don't watch or listen to the news at all for the next two weeks, unless this is absolutely critical for you to do so.

## Week Four

Continue to do your ten minutes as in Week Two.

Continue to do five minutes per session of visualisation as Week Three.

Now add five minutes of meditation at the end of each session.

## Meditation

As with all words, it's just a word until given form, structure and meaning. Meditation is sometimes confused with visualisation. It's sometimes considered as time spent concentrating on one particular thought, giving your complete and utter attention to the exclusion of all other thoughts. This is not meditation, as you saw last week, that's visualisation.

The best meaning I've seen is "meditation is the silence between the thoughts..."

To explain that a little further come with me in your mind back to where we met – in the supermarket. Follow me to the deli counter. In front of you now is the little ticket dispenser with numbered tickets and the electronic sign above our head says "Now serving No. 46" or something similar. Imagine that you pull a ticket and then you wander along the deli counter looking at the whole range of choices and you spend time deciding what you want.

You see the electronic counter flashes your number; you put your ticket in the bin and tell the assistant what you want. All pretty straightforward right? Now imagine standing back in front of the little ticket dispenser, this time as you pull a ticket you drop it straight into the bin and pull the next one and so on...

Why? I'll explain in a little while, stay with me a little longer.

As you continue pulling tickets quite rapidly to start with, in time, you start to slow down the number of tickets you pull but your aim in the bin is getting better as you are releasing the tickets. Soon there is space between the old ticket you release and the new one coming out of the machine.

This space is the silence and the tickets represent your thoughts.

Meditation is recognising a thought as it comes to mind but then releasing it as quickly as possible. Don't spend any time on that thought and, as your thoughts continue to come to mind, acknowledge their existence and let them go, just as if you were trying to catch a ball with slippery hands.

Thoughts will come thick and fast but with practise the thoughts start to diminish and the gaps become longer, because you are controlling them and not the other way around. Meditation is the silence between the thoughts.

Yours peacefully

Sue

# MY JOURNAL - WEEK 3

I've now arranged my schedule better and I'm more focused and have sorted out my priorities. At the end of this week I can definitely say that things are looking different.

I found this visualising thing hard to do. I started talking with one of my work colleagues who is into all the personal development stuff and he said, it's just like being a kid again, just start to use your imagination. First start off imagining some fun stuff you like to do, say bungee jumping off a cliff or sitting on a beautiful beach sipping a long cool drink.

Let your imagination run free for a while. Then when you are comfortable with that, start to focus on something you want to achieve, within a month or so, "or by this time next year I'll be.." use your imagination and talk about it as if it's happened already. Step into that car you always wanted, that new house on the beach, whatever it is for you. Have some fun. It's all there in your untapped imagination!

I started doing what he said, and loved it. I had to set an alarm to make sure that I only did five minutes. It's so easy to lose yourself when visualising, or, is it more true to say it's easy to find yourself when visualising?

My colleague at work loaned me a personal development book about visualisation techniques, which was very enlightening. There are many books available if you are interested to know more. My experience this week was that the more I played with these techniques the more my imagination was able to remove the boundaries that I had placed on it. Our imagination is too wide, too deep and too high for us to start to even chart the infinite options and possibilities held within. This has truly been a mind-blowing experience on so many levels.

## MY JOURNAL - WEEK 4

From the time I read Sue's email about Week Four I knew that this week would be the toughest part of this 30 day challenge. This process started as a gradual incline to take me from one level to another. Then came several big steps taking me higher in my understanding, to today, where I am more aware of my own spirit.

Growing up in the middle of England I'm aware that the West Midlands has a history of canals, in fact there are 160 miles of these canals in the area. This area is not known for being flat. It's just the opposite. In my imagination I can make water run uphill but in reality that's not going to happen. Canal locks allow a narrow boat or barge to travel up a waterway. This fantastic piece of engineering can, with very little effort, use the water released into the lock to raise the barge some considerable height allowing the boat to navigate on the higher level. This past 30 days has been a spirit lock that's had it's dam opened at one end and has been slowly raising me higher and higher each and every day so that I can now navigate through the higher levels.

When I read that I should meditate for five minutes three times a day, my first thought was of some guy sitting cross-legged going "Ommmm". I could not see me doing this either at home or in the office; they already think I'm going crazy saying out loud "No cheese Gromit" every 5 minutes.

The idea of silence between the thoughts is such an alien concept that I couldn't get my head around it. That was my problem; I was trying to get my head around something instead of letting go of the conscious thoughts.

There is a woman I see sometimes in the canteen and I've overheard her talking to her friend who meditates. So I had a word with her and she mentioned about relaxation meditation. This is when you stop thinking thoughts and focus on your breathing. I tried this and found with practise I could get into a good relaxation state; so good I fell asleep at times doing it, though thankfully not while I was at work.

Sitting at my PC at work I was copying some files when I noticed the graphic I was looking at and it reminded me of the concept of the silence between thoughts. When copying a file using Windows™

you see a graphic with a file at each end, during the copying process you see an animated piece of data transfer from one file to the other file.

This is the closest I've actually been to letting thoughts go as they appear. I'm tending to hold a thought for five or six seconds and then releasing it, as if it was like a piece of data on that copy screen animation. As with the copy screen graphic, as soon as one thought or piece of data has been released the next one is there. I have not at this stage been able to slow down my thoughts to any large degree. I assume it will require some more practice. I've agreed to give myself some space and also time to create this new way of thinking – or not thinking

Sue was right in her email to me. I have discovered that my life is more peaceful and less cluttered. I do feel like the dynamite stick has exploded through the possessions I had placed in the holes that were originally filled with peace and that the peace has returned to its rightful place. These 30 days have been a revelation and I'd recommend the process to anyone who feels like they want to get their life back under their control.

I met up with Sue; she said that having not seen me for 30 days she could see that I had actually had a shift in awareness during the period. She asked me if I noticed anything different in the supermarket. It was as if she could see through my eyes because I said, "Funny that you mention it, I do."

I had noticed that the supermarket seemed brighter. I had thought initially that they had either put brighter strip lighting in or they had replaced some defective strips. But there was more to it than that, it was as if all the colours of the displays had their colours enhanced, everything was more colourful. In fact everything looked like it had been polished, everything was gleaming.

But this wasn't just happening in the supermarket, I'd been noticing this for the past week all of the time, wherever I went. The best way I could describe this was, imagine that over time your eyesight has been getting progressively worse. You don't notice to start with but after time, edges of things get fuzzy, the definition goes. If you went to the optician and got your correct prescription you would see the difference immediately, objects would appear more defined, sharper and focussed. This is what I was experiencing now, all of the time.

Sue smiled and gave a knowing look and said, "I know you will enjoy the Personal Development day, you will get so much more from it now you are taking the peace."

Jim Parkes

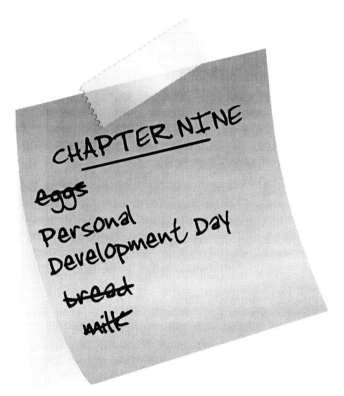

CHAPTER NINE

~~eggs~~

Personal
Development Day

~~bread~~

~~milk~~

It was a cold December Saturday morning but there was an excitement in the arena, I wouldn't have believed it if I hadn't been there. Over 1000 people packed into the hall to hear this celebrity personal development woman speak. It was like looking at a massive army, as we were all in uniform. The invitation stipulated that the dress code for the day would be white tee-shirt and blue jeans. The temperature outside was cold but inside the hall everyone was comfortable in this level of clothing.

As I walked through the crowd I heard people commenting about the dress code. Apparently, she always does this to breakdown any barriers between people. In this environment, no one knows who is a barrister and who is a barmaid.

The atmosphere was electric; there was a definite expectation that something really special was going to happen. There was upbeat music playing as more white tee-shirts entered the arena. An announcement was made that this event would start in five minutes so we should take our seats. The house lights were lowered and the stage lights lit.

"Ladies and gentlemen, we are proud to present to you, the world's leading expert in the field of personal development, please give her a warm welcome as she comes on stage." At that point the whole place went crazy, just like the film clips you've seen when the Beatles go on stage.

She too was dressed in a white tee-shirt and jeans. In her introduction she explained how the workers in the mid west wore denim as it was a strong material to take the rough and tumble of manual labour tasks. Today was going to be a day where there would be times when we would think and mull over new ideas and concepts. Times when we would be pulling down and demolishing thoughts, perceptions and limiting beliefs about ourselves. But most of all we would all walk out at the end of this day carrying a new mental toolbox filled with tools for us to use. We would be considering who we are and what we want out of life and how to get it. She also shared with us some "rules".

## GROUND RULES

1. We're all here for personal development so there would be times specifically for personal work and reflection and each individual would be given space they need to do that.

2. There would be group activity work, where you gain an insight into how others perceive you.

3. There would be collective group activities so you experience the effect of being part of a team of positively motivated people. Consider what that would be like for you at your place of work whether you are the boss or the worker.

4. We were there to enjoy not endure the day – so it was about having some fun!

## INTRODUCTION TO THE TOOLBOX

Any craft person will have at their disposal a toolbox where the tools of their trade are kept. Each tool has its own place within the box and each tool has a specific job to do. The toolbox is the location of where to find the tools you need.

We all know people who have a toolbox but the tools are scattered all over the place, so they never know where anything is and as a result the job takes that much longer. During the session we looked at the construction of the toolbox itself; identified the location of where you would keep it and made a commitment to leave it there ready for use.

She used a question: "If the light went out in your home would you know where your toolbox was with the torch inside?" Yes, you would if the toolbox remained in the same place, you could find it, even in the dark.

I couldn't fault the logic she was using, so I gave her the benefit of the doubt as she went on to a whole range of personal development issues.

## BEING CONGRUENT

A person is seen to be congruent when their desires, beliefs and attitude all align with each other and all pull together in the same direction. "Here we go again," I thought, the alignment of three aspects, everything of importance seems to come in threes. Just like you can be waiting for a bus for an eternity, and when you are just about to give up, three all come together.

Finding the peace box was good, but I needed Sue to explain, and now adding in the personal development element seems to have completed the picture for me.

This section made me sit up in my seat for another reason too. My job as a Database Administrator is normally referred to as a DBA. To be congruent was related to:

- Desire
- Belief
- Attitude

## Desire

She was looking here at the strong desires that we *want*, not just wishes but those things that are our main drivers. Desires that push us to get past the obstacles in our way.

She told the story of a young man who travelled a long way to meet a master in a particular field that the young man was interested in. On meeting this guru, the young man asked him what the secret was. The old man was silent but signalled the young man to follow him. On their journey, the young man continued to ask questions and the old man remained silent only to signal to keep following him. The old man stopped at a riverbank and signalled for the young man to enter the water. The young man walked into the water, the old man signalled for him to wade in until the water would have covered him if he didn't tread water to stay afloat. At this time the old man joined him and without a word the guru placed his hand on the young man's head and pushed him under the water.

The young man struggled to release his hand and come up for air, but to no avail. Sheer determination of the young man to preserve his life meant that after a number of failed attempts he was eventually free from the guru's hand and came to the surface gasping for air.

As he looked to the river's edge he saw the old man standing waiting for him. "What did you do that for?" asked the young man.

The old man said, "When you desire something as much as you desired the air to breathe when you were under the water, then you will be able the achieve anything you wish to achieve."

The young man walked away having learnt the lesson about desire.

### Belief

Initially, I thought she was going to talk about religious beliefs; instead this section was to do with personal beliefs, as in our own limiting beliefs of who we are and what we can do.

From the breakout sessions it was obvious that so many people believed something about themselves that was just not true any more. Even if they had been true for them at some point in their lives. Comments made to them as a child, such as "you'll never amount to much", or "you're useless, you are". The most popular one was from old school reports from over 10, 20 or 30 years ago saying "could do better".

If only people realised what lifetime damage these comments create they would be astonished, as I was as I listened to the people around me that day.

That section closed with a talk from the stage about how we can all do far more than we think we can. We can be far more than we think we can be and we can achieve remarkable things, if we only have belief in ourselves.

I smiled at one of the many exercises we did that day. She said she was going to say two words and we had to see what the words meant to us and what else they sparked off in our head. The two words were "Intel™ Inside". For me, I saw the rotating oval graphic followed closely behind by the sound of the chord and then the four notes that always accompanies the logo on the TV adverts.

She explained how clever this campaign was. When it was launched in 1991, it was cutting edge advertising. As far as Intel are concerned the computer can be of any brand, the importance is what's inside. "Intel™ Inside" was selling the quality of the microprocessor, the heart of the machine. What we have inside of us is far greater then the world's greatest microprocessor chip and we need to keep that in mind.

## Attitude

Attitude is everything. Without a good positive attitude where are we? This reminded me of one of the guys I know, who always says, "I love attitude, I eat, sleep and drink it". He helps people with their attitudes by running workshops on a regular basis.

He's right. Think of all the miserable people you know now, how would you describe their attitude? Now think of all the successful people you know or at least the ones you admire, even if you don't personally know them. How would you describe their attitude?

She talked about WIMP's – "Woe Is Me People", you know the type. They are dragging their problems around with them all the time. They always want to tell you how bad life is for them, how they have always been dealt the bad hand. There needs to be a shift in their attitude.

I found myself being carried away by all these concepts; it all seemed to make sense especially when considered side by side with what I'd learnt about peace. Most of the event was based around body and mind with the occasional skirting around the spirit aspect of the triad theory.

In the afternoon session we looked specifically at the tools to go into the toolbox.

Just to give you a tool-list, we looked at:

- Affirmations
- Visualisations
- Meditation
- Goal setting
- Dream boards
- Networks

Obviously, I had spent some time on the visualisation and meditation section so that wasn't new to me. The others were all new and below are the brief notes I made about these. But to be honest there are so many books about these subjects you may wish to buy one and read up on the subject.

### Affirmations

These are positive statements that are written down in the present tense about things that you want to happen, achieve or aspire to. These are read, and re-read on a daily basis.

The conscious mind makes judgements and knows the difference between reality and fantasy. On the other hand, the unconscious mind does not make judgements and will work to assist you to create positive steps towards your chosen statements.

Here's an example from a sales rep who currently aspires to be the Sales Manager in two years:

Affirmation: It's [date] and I am thrilled to be the new Sales Manager and I'm enjoying the [specific amount] per annum salary, and the respect of the current sales reps who admire the determination I have shown to achieve this position.

Affirmations can be for short, medium or long-term goals. The more specific and emotive the affirmation is, the better chance for achieving your desired results.

Use affirmations for every area of your life, not just business. Using affirmations in many areas of your life produces astounding results. Your mental attitude is paramount in health, wealth and stealth. In your education, creativity and your relationships. In summary, in all your hopes and dreams.

The most important aspect to remember is to write down your affirmations and read, and re-read them, both silently and out loud. There is power in hearing your own voice proclaiming these positive statements about your life.

## Goal Setting

Many people appreciate the need for goal setting and yet some don't take the time to carry out this activity. Set your goals and work out the stepping stones for how you will achieve those goals. Phrases used in this section were things like:

"If you fail to plan then (the result is) you plan to fail."

"Plan your attack and then attack your plan."

This was a fascinating session for me as this was very much delivered as a rigid determined pathway to tread. Set your goals and go for them with the mindset that you are an unstoppable force to be reckoned with. Push through obstacles, they are just tests to see how committed you are to achieve your goal.

Putting this alongside the PPS™ teaching I personally take an alternative view. I see that I need to set goals, this is the destination point on my internal satellite system and then I just push the button and my guidance system will plot the route. Having confidence that I'm now being guided I can enjoy the sights of the journey and also the people I meet along the way.

From the breakout sessions it was clear that there were some people with both eyes fixed on achieving their goal. They are a bit like the white rabbit in Alice in Wonderland, always saying "I'm late, I'm late, for a very important date". Always looking at what needs to be done. Surely, by fixing their sight purely on the goal set, they would always looking to the horizon and missing the daily pleasures. After all, it's the daily pleasures and the human interaction that constitutes our lives.

I put the famous John Lennon quote in my notebook; "Life is what happens to you while you are busy making other plans."

## Dream Boards

This is playtime for adults!

This is where we were all given a sheet of A3 paper and access to loads of magazines, scissors and glue and asked to identify all the things we wanted to achieve, acquire and do with our lives and write them down. Then we had to turn over the paper and with the use of the magazines find the items, or the closest we could and cut them and glue them onto paper. Once completed, we had our paper version of our dream board.

We were encouraged to take this basic "board" and develop it. To have an actual board somewhere that we can physically go to and place items we desire onto it. We should view it often.

The example was of a dream house; put the picture on the board, place actual photos of yourself (and those you love) next to the house, even cut out a window and place your photo inside as if you were literally looking out from the window. Then every time you look at that part of the board use your imagination to see what you would see as you are in that house NOW. How would you feel? What would the internal decorations be like? Put all the people inside the house you want to be with and imagine sitting down having a meal together. Experience the emotional attachment you would feel, live it, breath it, revel in it and most of all enjoy that moment. At an unconscious level your mind will work to help you to achieve your desire.

## Networks

The power is within networks. We considered TV networks and all of the public utilities. A massive matrix that covers a whole geographical area. Connectivity on this scale brings the powerhouse together. Each individual section has its own part to play for the effectiveness of the network. And the whole structure is held together by the connections between each other. Individual sections may not be considered as important, but each is vital and is part of the designer's master blue print. There is no difference when we look at ourselves and the people around us.

What we can achieve individually is outstanding, if we were to only put our mind to it. Together, there is incredible scope in the networks for the good of a group, a community, a country or mankind itself.

During the break I went to the bookstall at the back of the arena. I was amazed by the number of personal development books that are available. One of the banners I saw made me smile, it read: "It's not how many books you can get through, it's how many books get through to you." More and more, people are searching for answers, searching for a different reality for themselves. As I looked around the arena I couldn't help notice that there seemed to be a lack of peace. There were plenty of "rah-rah" people, you know the ones punching the air saying, "Yes, I can fly", but there was a distinct lack of peace in the room.

It was a long day, which ended dramatically with over one thousand people doing a fire walk. People walking barefoot over hot coals at an average temperature of 1200 degrees Fahrenheit without getting burnt. The message is simple: If you can walk over hot coals what else is it possible for you to do? Go out and be the best you can. I went into this day a sceptic but I came out a true believer in personal development.

To sum up the personal development day it would be fair to say the words of Abraham Lincoln sprang to mind; "If I had eight hours to cut down a tree I'd spend seven hours sharpening my axe". Personal development from my brief introduction is all about preparing the person to accept that their current reality may only be one option. There are many more options and choices. I can choose to stay where I am, or I can look to find an alternative.

The alternatives exist if I take the time to sharpen my axe.

Jim Parkes

As the Christmas festivities drew closer, trips to the supermarkets were in full swing. Aisles bursting with people frantically stocking up like squirrels, hoarding up provisions for a long hard winter period. It's hard to understand what is actually going through the shopper's minds. After all, the shop would only close for a maximum of three days that year. Observing the strategy of your average shopper you would be convinced that they will not be able to get provisions for a least a month.

In a vain attempt to calm shoppers, holiday music was being piped through the store. This strategy worked during the latter part of November, but now well into the second week in December it was a little grating on the nerves. A one-way system had been introduced around the store and first aiders, including the fork lift truck driver, were on standby in the likely event of customer scuffles breaking out of which there are several around the store at any particular moment. Like the folks who are fighting in the bread aisle over the last thick sliced in the whole store.

An unfair duel was taking place between two pensioners, one with a baguette and the other with a two day old French stick left marooned due to its particularly hard exterior. Both were being egged on by a group of kids shouting "fight, fight, fight". Suddenly the store SWAT team entered the picture. They assessed the situation and took swift action – they called for backup! The backup teams were already engaged in other incidents around the store and therefore couldn't assist. I continued on my travels leaving behind the ensuing carnage.

I passed a mother with a young boy who was very busy while his mother was in deep conversation with her friend. He attempted to find the best possible toy from within the inside of the Christmas crackers. His small fingers were just the right size to fish out the toys without having to pull the crackers. He had an assortment of plastic hair slides, combs, false moustaches and rings and a mountain of discarded crackers all around him, and his mother was oblivious to it all.

As I turned into aisle 13 I had the shock of my life, the peace boxes had all gone. In fact it was worse than that, the space where they were had been filled with additional seasonal CDs. I wondered how many more CDs could possibly be the best ever... of anything any more.

This felt like a sharp slap in the face to me. So stunned was I that I asked an assistant about the peace in a box and his reply was like receiving a second slap. "Sorry, there's no peace now until after Christmas."

Isn't it ironic, at this time of year, the season of peace and goodwill towards all men, there is no peace to be found. No space to be found on the shelves for this precious gift that we all are craving in our lives. Then, just when I was feeling low, I felt someone tap me on the shoulder. As I turned around Sue was there, holding a beautifully wrapped Christmas present with a tag that said: "To my dear friend Thomas, may you doubt no more. Merry Christmas – with love from Sue xxx"

The hustle and bustle of the surroundings disappeared as I looked into her peaceful eyes I smiled and said, "Thank you."

"Go on, open it!" she said. Like a child I ripped open the paper to reveal an individual portion of peace in a box. I hugged Sue and beamed, "Thank you so much, how can I ever repay you for all you have shown me?"

Sue said, "Continue being a peacetaker and share with as many people as possible the knowledge I have shared with you." She kissed me and said "Merry Christmas... see you next week."

I have kept my promise to Sue that I would tell as many people as possible about my experience of peace in a box. My story is now told but my journey has only just begun.

The macro and micro analogies continue to reveal themselves through the weekly messages I receive in the peace boxes and also through Sue, who is now my very special friend. Both of these sources are precious to me now, and I will continue to be a peacetaker for the whole of my lifetime.

Through the pages of this book you have travelled along with me on my journey as my companion, as a silent observer, seeing my mistakes and in your heart knowing that you would make a better job than I have. I too have been aware of your unseen presence with me and through the pages, I have experienced a kindred spirit draw alongside me as I wrote this account. We have laughed and cried together on this emotional adventure, and along the way, we have shared and taken the peace together.

It is my belief that this joining together of author and reader is possible because our spirits and peace itself are not bound in time, they exist outside of that dimension and therefore past, present and future are not relevant. As I wrote this book I felt your travelling companionship with me every step of the way.

Whether we meet in person or not, I truly believe our spirits have shared a part of the road of life together and for that I am grateful to you, my friend. Someone sent me an email sometime ago entitled "A Reason, A Season or A Lifetime" which I would like to give to you as a present to conclude this story. You will see the text on the following page and as you read it consider your interaction with the people who are part of your world.

Finally, I ask you reader, if you know of any lawful reason why you should not join me in being proactive in achieving peace in your life and in those around you that you speak now or forever hold your peace (in a box).

## A Reason, a Season, or a Lifetime

People come into your life for a reason, a season, or a lifetime. When you figure out which one it is, you will know what to do for each person.

When someone is in your life for a REASON . . . It is usually to meet a need you have expressed. They have come to assist you through a difficulty, to provide you with guidance and support, to aid you physically, emotionally, or spiritually. They may seem like a godsend, and they are! They are there for the reason you need them to be.

Then, without any wrong doing on your part, or at an inconvenient time, this person will say or do something to bring the relationship to an end.

Sometimes they die.

Sometimes they walk away.

Sometimes they act up and force you to take a stand.

What we must realise is that our need has been met, our desire fulfilled, their work is done. The prayer you sent up has been answered.

And now it is time to move on.

When people come into your life for a SEASON . . .

Because your turn has come to share, grow, or learn.

They bring you an experience of peace, or make you laugh.

They may teach you something you have never done.

They usually give you an unbelievable amount of joy.

Believe it! It is real! But, only for a season.

LIFETIME relationships teach you lifetime lessons; things you must build upon in order to have a solid emotional foundation. Your job is to accept the lesson, love the person, and put what you have learned to use in all other relationships and areas of your life. It is said that love is blind but friendship is clairvoyant.

Author Unknown

# THE KEY MESSAGE AND A FUN EXERCISE

What you will need:

- This book (of course)!
- A pencil (that needs sharpening)
- A pencil sharpener
- A quiet, comfortable place to sit or lie
- A few minutes to spare

Look at the pencil. You can see that it has three distinct components. There's the outer case, this may be coloured, then a soft inner wood and finally the lead, or more accurately it's a carbon based material at its core.

We are made up of three components

- Body – our outer case, this may be coloured
- Mind – a soft pliable material
- Spirit – soul, inner self, the real you – your core

Take a moment to relax, close your eyes and take three good breaths in and exhale slowly and fully between each.

Take a moment to think about the analogy between a pencil and yourself, then...

Take a moment to consider how you are actually feeling right now, emotionally.

Now read on...

As with a pencil, if you put these three components together, body, mind and spirit (your PPS™), and focus on a task there is the potential to create a masterpiece limited only by the mind of the designer, author, composer etc...

Remember the time as a child you sharpened a pencil until you had a point as sharp as a scalpel only to find that because you had dropped the pencil many times that you'd broken all the lead and the point would fall out every time and you'd have to start again?

Want more fulfilment and peace in your life? It's all about getting your body, mind and spirit working together in synergy to achieve your goals in life.

Whether you have arrived at this page after reading the whole book or from just turning here from the contents page I now want to give you a task to perform. As a multi-sensory experience take your pencil and sharpen it and without having to complete a risk assessment form, just apply a gentle amount of pressure on one of your finger tips with the pencil point.

Concentrate on the sensation you are feeling in that finger and ask yourself this question: "If I could focus my whole-self, body, mind and spirit as this pencil is focused now, what one area in my life would there be a possibility I could change for the better?" That could be for you, gaining more self esteem, self worth or self belief or a more fulfilling relationship with a partner, or business colleague or business venture.

Well done! Now why not reward your whole-self by taking a few moments to turn the clock back to your favourite junior classroom or teacher. First of all, in your mind's eye, select your childhood good memories DVD, and then go to the "select scenes" screen, choose the scene now as you push the button see the classroom build in your mind.

First, picture the classroom door, now open the door and walk inside, see the windows, blackboard, smell the chalk dust cloud as your teacher wipes the board. See the desk, is it one of the desks with an ink pot holder and a groove on the front for your pencils? Run your finger along the whole length of the groove. Lift your desk lid, is it tidy inside? Slam the lid shut loudly for fun.

Now, picture your exercise book in front of you. Your best friend is smiling at you and you are enjoying the lesson together.

Now physically take the pencil you have just sharpened and carefully hold it next to your nose (don't push it up your nose). Close your eyes and take a few deep, long breaths in and enjoy the smell of the freshly sharpened pencil then and for a few moments allow your whole-self to fully experience that pleasant classroom setting again.

As you return back to your present comfortable space, notice the physical aspect of where you are now, the door, the window etc. and when you are fully back into that place, consider how that experience was for you.

How are you feeling now – are you more restful, more peaceful after you have taken some time out from your hectic life and spent some time reflecting? You have now completed your first peace taking experience and you can now answer, "YES" to the question "seriously, are you taking the peace?"

# SUGGESTED FURTHER READING

Chopra, D  The Book Of Secrets, Rider Publishing an imprint of Ebury Press

Dwoskin, H  The Sedona Method   Sedona Press

Eckhart, T   The Power Of Now   Hodder and Stoughton a division of Hodder Headline

Johnson, S  Who Moved My Cheese?  Vermilion an imprint of Ebury Press

Murphy, J  The Power Of Your Subconscious Mind Simon & Schuster UK Ltd

Persaud, R  The Motivated Mind , Bantam Press

Rohn, J  7 Strategies For Wealth & Happiness  Prima Publishing

Schwartz, D.J  The Magic Of Thinking Big, Simon & Schuster UK Ltd

Sharma, R.S   The Monk Who Sold His Ferrari  Element an imprint of Harper Collins Publishers Ltd

# ABOUT THE AUTHOR

September 11 2001 was the catalyst for change. It was at that point that Jim realised that he was not following his true destiny in life. This was the start of a three year journey into making life changing decisions. He was introduced to the concepts of Personal Development in 2003 and then finally, in March 2004 after working 27 years in corporate life for a large utility company he realised that there was so much more that he was supposed to be doing with his life. Since then he has never looked back and life has taken Jim into new and exciting (ad)ventures.

"Seriously, Are You Taking The Peace?" Is the first novel from the author and his unique style of writing has a wide appeal to those who are new to the concepts of Personal Development, self-awareness and expression.

Over the past two years Jim has become a multi-sensory professional speaker having recently discovered his latent creativity and started to play again with his imagination.

"... the dreams that you dare to dream, really do come true"

Taken from the song "Somewhere over the Rainbow" Lyrics by E.Y. Harburg

# BIOGRAPHY OF JIM PARKES

### 11th January 1960

He was born at an early age, actually 3 months premature to be precise. That was probably the first and only time he has ever been early. There is fashionably late and then there's the "late Jim Parkes".

As a kid growing up he wanted to be many things and many people from a train driver to an astronaut, Star Trek's James T Kirk to John Travolta in Saturday Night Fever. However, it didn't help that the warp-drive hadn't been invented or he couldn't dance.

He loved drama but was never good enough to be picked for school plays. He was always the one left standing by the wall when all the parts had been dished out.

School reports were consistent, with the words "could do better" featuring prominently.

### June 1976

He left full time education in June 1976 and enjoyed one of the best summers on record taking a "well earned break" – his words.

## September 1976

He fell into corporate life at the tender age of 16 and continued to free fall down that long rabbit hole for 27 years before emerging back into the big wide world again in April 2004. "There's life Jim, but not as you know it!"

## April 2004

He started on a journey of self-discovery, awareness and personal development. His "continuing mission" is to "baldly go" further into these areas, to discover and live his true purpose in life.

After kicking his heels for a time and staring at his navel for inspiration he decided he would return to his first love, that of being on a stage. However, this time he would be *speaking* in public. Shock and horror, people actually enjoyed listening to him.

Normally words like, "multi-sensory experience", "inspirational", "thought provoking" are used after hearing him speak.

On one occasion, someone said: "He has a voice that would be good for a 'closed eye technique'". Translated into English that actually means, "He sends people to sleep!"

Who knows the truth? Only those who have heard him speak I guess.

It's said that Jim is a "people person", willing to give a listening ear to those who need it.

## ChildLine

His passion to help distressed children and young people led him to be a ChildLine counsellor at the Birmingham base for a while. Although no longer on the phones he is an active fundraiser for this incredible charity who celebrate their 20th Birthday in 2006.

## January 2006

He set a goal of writing his first novel to share his thoughts on how to get some peace back into our lives.

## September 2006

"Seriously, are you taking the peace?" is published.

## You Decide

You now have an overview of this new author; it's up to you to decide whether you like this man or not. As you can see, throughout his life he has had many failures, and he will be the first to tell you that he will have many more. However, he will keep getting up, dusting himself off and will have another go.

# Get Your Exclusive "Peace In A Box" Audio Bonuses

To download your FREE and exclusive "Peace In A Box" bonuses just visit the link below and complete the form.

Get "Peace In A Box" now at...
**www.BookShaker.com/peace**

Printed in the United Kingdom
by Lightning Source UK Ltd.
132739UK00001B/88/A